"I really should get to work."

Juliet sighed and started to move off the barstool, but Cole stopped her with a hand on her thigh.

"Don't tell me you have another job tonight." The thought of her leaving the party was enough to ruin his birthday. He had to do something to keep her here.

"I just need to help—" she started to say, but he gave in to the impulse to lean over and kiss her.

Under normal circumstances, he wouldn't have kissed her so quickly. But the way she kissed made him glad he had. He barely suppressed a groan of pleasure when she snaked her arm around his neck and coaxed his tongue into an erotic dance.

The feel of her too-soft lips, the taste of her, the tempting boldness of her tongue—he'd never forget these sensations.

He wanted her so badly he could hardly breathe. Wanted to touch, explore, taste... He wanted their bodies tangled together until morning.

She broke the kiss and trailed her tongue along his jaw, her breath tickling his skin along the way. "You have a room here at the hotel tonight, right?"

Cole managed to nod.

"Then let's go."

Dear Reader,

This book is my tribute to scandalous women everywhere—those who flaunt their outrageous ways, and the rest of us, who keep our wild sides hidden under nice-girl exteriors!

The League of Scandalous Women is a product of my imagination—though I couldn't resist doing a little spin-off from the title of a recent movie when I came up with the name—and it's a group I'd love to be a part of. Women who dare to defy convention, dare to be themselves, dare to go after what they really want in life, are the kind of women I admire most.

Much as I loved writing about Juliet and Cole's steamy romance, I had just as much fun writing about Delia. If this book is my tribute to scandalous women, then Delia is my tribute to the scandalous women who have settled down. Women like her are the backbones of society, and I am blessed with many Delias in my life. My wish for all of them is that they get their own maid service and an occasional romp in the back of the family vehicle!

I love to hear from readers, so drop me a note to let me know what you think of *Some Kind of Sexy*. You can reach me via e-mail at jamie@jamiesobrato.com or surf on over to my Web site, www.jamiesobrato.com to learn more about me and my upcoming books.

Sincerely,

Jamie Sobrato

Books by Jamie Sobrato

SOME KIND OF SEXY

Jamie Sobrato

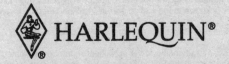

TORONTO • NEW YORK • LONDON
AMSTERDAM • PARIS • SYDNEY • HAMBURG
STOCKHOLM • ATHENS • TOKYO • MILAN • MADRID
PRAGUE • WARSAW • BUDAPEST • AUCKLAND

To Cindy Procter-King,
my dear friend and critique partner—
and one of my favorite scandalous women.

ISBN 0-373-79137-2

SOME KIND OF SEXY

Copyright © 2004 by Jamie Sobrato.

Prologue

JULIET EMORY HELD the leather diary on her lap, both curious about and afraid of the secrets it kept. She had been saving her aunt's diary for months, waiting for the right time to read it. There would never be a right time though. It was the diary of her only family member, her beloved aunt Ophelia who had raised her from the time she was a little girl and who had passed away four months ago.

She needed to hang on to this piece of Ophelia, and now was as good a time as any. Yet when she imagined reading the diary, she felt like a voyeur. Her aunt had shown her the side of herself she wanted Juliet to know, but what if reading the journal revealed parts of Ophelia that were best kept hidden?

Juliet didn't want the image of her greatest role model tarnished, and yet she wanted to hear Ophelia's voice again, even if only in print.

A breeze rustled the leaves of the trees in the garden, reminding Juliet of how she'd sat in this very spot in the gazebo under the vines of bougainvillea as a child, imagining that the trees were whispering to her, that fairies flitted about among the flowers and that all her dreams were possible.

She opened the journal and a paper fell out and landed

at her feet. A small, yellowed piece of parchment paper, which she bent and picked up.

She unfolded it and read the typed title.

Guiding Principles of The League of Scandalous Women.

A flood of memories came rushing at Juliet. Her aunt's Garden District mansion had been a center of the New Orleans art scene at one time, and The League of Scandalous Women had been at the heart of it all.

Any woman who felt bound by society's restrictions, any woman who wanted to celebrate self-expression, any woman who dared to defy the roles handed to her was welcome, and Juliet had witnessed it all through the wide eyes of a child.

She'd overheard the intellectual debates, the discussions of sexual freedom for women and the poetry readings that had often gone on into the early hours of the morning. She'd sat on the knees of some of the progressive thinkers who'd shaped the future for women in America. She'd grown up thinking avant-garde was normal.

As she read the list of the league's guiding principles, she was amazed at how well they still applied today. Aunt Ophelia and her friends had been ahead of their time, and all the things they'd tried to drill into her when she was growing up—ideas she'd rolled her eyes at and ignored—seemed revolutionary, even from her jaded twenty-first century perspective.

She re-read the list, then carefully folded the paper again and placed it inside the journal, too thrilled by this brush with the past to read more now. She felt energized and excited, not sure what she'd do with those guiding principles, but sure she needed to do something. Her gut told her it would be something big.

Something revolutionary. Something scandalous.

1

The League of Scandalous Women's Guiding Principle 1:
A scandalous woman knows that brazenness is a virtue.

"I'VE BEEN A BAD, bad girl."

Juliet smiled as she held the phone to her ear, relieved to hear her best friend's voice after two weeks. "I'm guessing Cancun will never be the same."

"Actually, you'd be surprised how little partying I did." Rebecca Wilson laughed. "I spent most of my vacation inside a hotel suite."

"Ah, so you met a bad, bad boy to burn your energy with."

"Not just any bad boy," Rebecca said in a tone so pregnant with meaning that Juliet got a sick feeling in her stomach for reasons she couldn't have explained.

"I'm listening."

"Are you sitting down?"

"Yes." Kicked back in her office chair with her feet propped up on a desk littered with party supplies, to be exact.

The inexplicable sick feeling grew.

"I'm getting married!"

Juliet expelled a sigh of relief. This was clearly one of Rebecca's silly practical jokes, and not even a funny one.

The idea of wild, crazy, happily single Rebecca getting hitched was about as believable as Juliet volunteering to join a convent.

"Oh, that's great, because I have Brad Pitt tied up in my basement. We can make it a double wedding after I force him to divorce Jennifer."

Silence on the line. And then Rebecca said, "Juliet, I'm serious. I met a guy in Mexico. He was on vacation, too. He lives in San Diego, and we're getting married."

Oh.

"This is just so…sudden," Juliet said, fully aware that she sounded more like a worried mother than a supportive friend. "Are you sure about this guy?"

"Of course I'm sure! Wait till you meet him—he's just fabulous."

Rebecca sounded dreamier than Juliet had ever heard her, and all she could muster in response was a feeble, "Wow."

"I shouldn't be telling you this over the phone, but I wanted to share the news immediately, and I know how your schedule is."

"It's okay." Juliet forced herself to smile so that she'd sound cheery. "We'll get together and have a celebratory drink soon."

"Absolutely, but I have to ask you now—will you be my maid of honor?"

Juliet winced, when she knew she should have felt touched. "Of course I will."

"Great. I'm already thinking about what I want the dresses to look like…."

She continued to hear Rebecca's voice, but the words stopped registering as the sick feeling grew into a full-blown case of nausea. She should have been happy about her best friend's marriage announcement. She had no problem with the institution of marriage. She considered it a perfectly fine expression of the love between man and woman.

What she disliked was all of her party crowd slowly dwindling to nothing thanks to marriage and the inevitable children that followed.

And now Rebecca, too.

If she wasn't careful, she'd find herself hanging out with the perennial nightclub lizards, the aging men and women who trolled all the hot night spots endlessly in search of a good time. Oh hell, who was she kidding—if she wasn't careful, she'd end up being one of those pitiable souls, decked out in last year's fashions and inhaling froufrou drinks by the dozen.

She'd never expected to be the last girl standing, and yet here she was, forced to swallow the news that her best friend and favorite party girl was finally getting married, leaving Juliet as the last single in their former crowd.

"Jule, you still there?"

Juliet adjusted the phone and swallowed the lump in her throat. Okay, she was supposed to sound happy, make giddy exclamations of matrimonial joy.

"Yes, I'm just in shock."

"I'd love for you to help me with the wedding arrangements."

"Of course. I'd be happy to help." Happy like she felt when she was twelve and her dog ran away.

"I want it to be an unforgettable day. Great food, great music, great atmosphere, and I know no one can throw a party better than you."

Juliet made a face at the phone, feeling guilty even as

she did it. She just needed to shake off the lousy attitude and be happy for Rebecca.

She forced herself to smile again. "I'm all booked up this weekend. Why don't we plan to meet for lunch before Audrey's baby shower and discuss all the details?"

Audrey was yet another one of their former party friends who'd succumbed to the lure of marriage and kids.

"Is something wrong? You sound like you're upset."

"No, no, I'm thrilled for you. I just got a stack of bills from my aunt's estate right before you called." That part, at least, was true.

"Oh sweetie, I'm sorry. It's hard enough to have her pass away so suddenly, let alone have to deal with all the details of the estate on your own."

"I'll manage," Juliet said, and she had managed so far, but if the bills kept piling up, she was pretty sure she'd start having murderous feelings toward the mailman.

"So I'll see you Saturday after next, around noon?"

"At Ruby Q's?"

"Sounds good."

Juliet hung up the phone and buried her face in her hands, expelling a ragged sigh as she did so. Before her eyes, her close circle of girlfriends had been reduced to nothing. They were the friends she'd relied on, friends she considered family, since she didn't have any blood relatives of her own left. One by one they'd gotten married, had kids, and their girlfriend time invariably disappeared. Now it would happen to Rebecca, too.

Who would she go out clubbing with? Who would tell her when her dress was too short or her shoes didn't work with her outfit? Who would help her get rid of losers that couldn't understand why she wasn't interested?

Juliet had spent her twenties shopping, hanging out and partying with her friends, and some silly part of her had actually believed the party would never end. She'd been foolish enough to think that at least a few of her friends, like her, didn't want to settle down anytime soon. Now it seemed as if she was destined to go out alone every Saturday night, have the traditional Sunday girlfriend brunch by herself and be the awkward third wheel whenever her formerly single friends invited her over for dinner.

With a deep, cleansing breath, she vowed to stop feeling sorry for herself, and turned her attention to the stack of bills that had just arrived in the mail. Aunt Ophelia might have passed away four months ago, but her recent and entirely uncharacteristic obsession with buying junk through the mail lived on.

Juliet was about to write a check to pay for a two-hundred-dollar fruit juicer when the sound of the front door caught her attention. She looked up to see a six-foot-high wall of solid muscle clad in black leather standing across from her desk. Juliet immediately recognized him as Max Matheson, one of the three brothers who'd hired her last week to throw a surprise thirtieth birthday bash for their youngest brother.

"Hi, Max."

"Hi." He flashed a smile that caused Juliet a pang of disappointment over the wedding ring he wore. "Just stopped by to drop off the stuff you asked for. Sorry I'm a little late."

More than a little, considering the party was tomorrow night, and she still had to scan the photos he'd brought and make party decorations from them.

But Juliet had learned long ago that the customer was

always right, even when he was dead wrong, so she smiled and said, "No problem. I was just about to confirm the entertainment. Once I get these photos ready, everything should be set for tomorrow."

He didn't need to know that the entertainment had just canceled because of a nasty flu bug. Juliet didn't believe in unnecessarily upsetting the customer.

"Cole's gonna love it. Thanks for all your help on this."

She watched as the oldest brother of the Matheson clan disappeared out the front door of Any Occasion. On the street outside, midafternoon traffic was light, and lunchtime shoppers and tourists strolled by. A few paused to look at the window display that advertised Juliet's party-planning business, but most passed the run-down storefront without a second glance. She needed to find a new location, but good business space was hard to find in New Orleans, and while Any Occasion turned a decent profit, she certainly didn't earn enough money to pay the high rent most of the places she liked were commanding.

She frowned as she opened up the bag Max had left her, then pulled out a stack of photos, newspaper clippings and a yearbook.

The top photo of a gorgeous hunk of male with wavy brown hair sitting at a picnic table holding a beer and laughing, took her breath away. This was Cole Matheson, the birthday boy.

Ay Carumba.

His laughing blue eyes managed to convey both warmth and cool sensuality, and his jawline, darkened by a few days' growth of beard, begged for a woman's touch.

She began flipping through the photos, one gorgeous shot after another. Cole in high school, Cole in college, Cole hanging out with his brothers—little brother Cole was the hottest guy she'd laid eyes on in a long, long time.

Juliet squirmed in her chair as she admired a photo of him climbing out of a swimming pool, his hair slicked back and his tanned honey skin glistening in the sun.

A wild night with a babe like Cole was just what she needed to take her mind off of her problems and cure her of her bad attitude about Rebecca's engagement.

She dug around in her memory of the last conversation she'd had with Cole's brothers for any mention of whether he was single or taken. They had mentioned him being a wild, partying bachelor…. Yes, they'd definitely mentioned inviting his single female friends.

Surely she could find some time during the party tomorrow night to put out feelers, do some flirting and see what came of it. Who knew—maybe she really would hook up with the sexy birthday boy.

Juliet forced herself to focus on work again. She brought up the address book on her computer and found the phone number for Risky Business exotic dancers. The Matheson brothers had been very specific in their wish for a stripper to entertain their brother, and hey, nothing loosened up a party like a woman taking her clothes off.

Juliet herself had been known to stir things up at parties on occasion by strategically removing an item of clothing or two. Secretly, she'd always had a fantasy about doing a striptease for a deserving male, maybe even in front of an audience, and as she began dialing the number for Risky Business, a wicked little idea formed in her head.

Maybe she wouldn't need their services after all….

No, she couldn't.

Or could she?

Juliet glanced down at a photo of Cole on her desk, and a warm, fuzzy feeling formed between her legs. If her life needed a shake-up right now, pretending to be a stripper was about as shaky as she could get.

COLE MATHESON HATED PARTIES. Hated the loud music, hated the crowds, hated the often-forced merriment, hated the way it was impossible to carry on more than the shallowest conversation when bass-thumping music was roaring out of speakers from every direction and pounding all coherent thought from his brain.

This, however, was a party he had to at least try to enjoy. His brothers had thrown this one for him to celebrate his thirtieth birthday, and he knew they'd had good intentions. So he tossed back his third shot of Wild Turkey and smiled like he was enjoying himself.

In a few minutes, thanks to the smooth, sultry effect of the whiskey, he no longer had to pretend. He normally wouldn't have condoned heavy drinking to dull the edges of any experience, but these were special circumstances.

After all, he was turning thirty. He never thought he'd get hung up on his own age, but all day today he'd found himself returning to the fact that his life wasn't playing out like he'd thought it would. He'd always pictured himself settling down by thirty, playing baseball with his kids by forty.... He was getting way ahead of himself, considering he didn't have a steady girlfriend or even the prospect of one in sight. It must have been the whiskey doing the thinking.

"Hey, bro. I think I saw Jeannie Monroe a few minutes ago." Paul clapped him on the back. "Want me to send her over here?"

Jeannie was a long-ago ex-girlfriend who'd gone away to grad school, thus ending their relationship, and forever after his well-intentioned but meddling family had branded her The One That Got Away. She may have gotten away, but she certainly hadn't felt like The One.

Cole had an odd feeling this whole night might have been orchestrated to give him another chance with Jeannie. If so, his brothers'—or more likely his sisters-in-law's— efforts were wasted.

"We've got a little surprise coming up shortly."

"I'm afraid to ask."

"Don't bother, because I won't give you any clues, except to say you're gonna love it."

Cole gave his brother what he meant as a wry look, but a haze had settled over his brain, and he couldn't quite be sure he had complete control of his facial muscles.

His brother wandered off, and then a cute blonde whose name he couldn't remember sat down next to him. He was pretty sure she was a friend of his sister-in-law Delia, and he was also pretty sure he was supposed to know her name, but that's the best he could do. He glanced down at her smooth, athletic legs below her miniskirt, but they didn't jar his memory.

"Wasn't it great of your brothers to throw this party for you?"

"Yeah, great." Just freaking great.

"Delia told me you're an organic psychologist."

Organizational psychologist. Normally he would have corrected her right away, but tonight he was feeling like a wiseass.

"Yeah, I grow all-natural vegetables and then help them

work through their emotional issues,'' he said with a straight face.

His companion seemed to give the matter some thought. ''Wow, who pays you to do *that?*''

It was going to be a long, long night if this conversation kept going.

''The organic food industry. If you'll excuse me, I need to find someone.''

Someone, as in Delia, to make sure she understood that he was not interested in having his family choose his dates for him.

Cole wandered around the room and onto the balcony, where he found his sister-in-law gazing up at the sky on what was a rare, clear night in New Orleans. He looked up, too, but his equilibrium was a little off. He wavered to the side and caught his balance with a hand on the balcony railing.

''I hope you're not making a wish for me to fall for one of your friends.''

Delia turned and smiled. ''Of course not. I was making a wish that I'll be able to eat that chocolate cake in there without having to go to the gym tomorrow to work it off.''

''Could you please stop the matchmaking? Is that too much to ask?''

''I didn't send Cammie over there. She wanted to talk to you.''

''She thinks I'm an organic psychologist who counsels vegetables.''

''Okay, okay. She's not very bright, but she's pretty.''

Cole gave her a look.

Delia sighed. ''I'll try not to send anyone else in your direction.''

"Thanks. Just remember, I don't need any help with my love life."

Delia cast a skeptical look at him but didn't argue.

Ten minutes later, he'd downed another shot, and he'd even begun to enjoy the too-loud music, when someone shut it off.

Cole looked up from his shot glass to see his oldest brother, Max, standing on top of the bar in the rented hotel suite. Conversation died as people waited to hear what he had to say.

"We all know why we're here tonight, right?"

A general "whoo-hooo" erupted in the crowd, and Max waited for everyone to quiet down before continuing.

"That's right, our little brother turns thirty today!"

"Little brother" was a moniker Cole had accepted he'd never outlive, but that didn't mean he had to like it. He'd earned his doctorate in psychology by the time most people were just starting grad school, run the Boston marathon, climbed Mount McKinley and beaten all three of his brothers at poker countless times, but none of that mattered to them.

To Paul, Max and Jake, he was the same little pest who'd followed them around for years trying to join in their big-kid games. They'd never see him as an adult, even when he was old and gray.

"I have to admit," Max continued, "I'm a little concerned about Cole lately. He's in the midst of his eligible bachelor days, but he doesn't seem to be enjoying them nearly as much as he should, if you know what I mean."

A few people who'd had possibly even more to drink than Cole whooped and yelled "Yeah!"

Cole tried not to roll his eyes. His brothers, who were

all married now, were forever commenting on how he should have been out chasing every woman he saw, but that wasn't Cole's style. He liked getting to know a woman, developing a real relationship with her. He just hadn't found The One yet.

And then there were his brothers' wives, whom he loved dearly, but who all shared a seriously annoying matchmaking streak. He would have bet anything they were the reason Jeannie Monroe and more than a few single friends of theirs were present tonight.

"It's all work and no play for our little brother, but we're hoping to change that tonight. So, friends, I propose a toast." Max hefted his beer in the air, just as a loud knock sounded on the door of the suite. "Uh-oh, who could that be?"

Whatever his brothers were up to, Cole had a feeling he wasn't going to like it.

His brother Paul opened the door, and at that moment a bass-laden groove erupted from the speakers, something raunchy with an irresistible dance beat.

"Looks like we have a guest."

Cole caught sight of the "guest." A woman in what looked to be a female Zorro outfit strutted into the suite, and the music stopped again.

She halted in the middle of the room, where the crowd had cleared out, raised her whip, and cracked it in the air. The men in the audience whistled and howled. She looked slowly around the room until her gaze settled on Cole, and then he knew she wasn't just an eccentrically dressed guest.

He took in the sight of Miss Zorro, her long chestnut hair draping her shoulders in a silken curtain, her face obscured by a black mask. He could see only her eyes, which were large and brown, and her mouth, lush and red.

She wore a black bolero hat and a black cape over a skin-tight black leather dress that was entirely unsuited for horseback riding, and her high-heeled boots accented a pair of long, thin legs that screamed pinup girl. His gaze had just settled on the delicious peaks of her breasts straining against the dress when the music started again, and she began to dance.

That was when it became clear to him that his brothers had hired him a stripper. And if he hadn't been so mesmerized by the sway of her hips, he might have been able to muster a little annoyance. Not that he didn't appreciate a beautiful woman taking her clothes off, but he usually preferred that it happen behind closed doors rather than in front of fifty of his closest friends.

Cole felt his body temperature rise as she danced provocatively around him, her hips gyrating left and right to the beat of the music. She was close enough to touch without actually brushing up against him, and then she pulled up a chair, inviting him with the motion of her hand to sit.

He did as asked without thinking twice. Even under the influence of too much whiskey, he knew he was getting the show of his life.

She twirled around and sent her cape billowing over his head, then tossed her hat into the crowd. Standing with her legs spread wide, she continued moving her hips to the beat, taunting Cole with her whip, hypnotizing him with each delicious move.

In his hypnotic state, he still managed to imagine exactly what he would have loved to do with the sexy stripper.

He'd show her a few erotic uses for that whip, among other things....

He was vaguely aware that she took off the cape and tossed it aside, but his attention was riveted to her when she managed to remove her dress, oh-so-slowly unzipping it down the front, while she had one foot propped between his legs on the chair. She slid the dress off her shoulders and flung it aside, but Cole never saw where it landed. He was too mesmerized by the sight of her round, perfect breasts encased in a black leather bra to notice.

And as she gyrated to the beat, his gaze traveled down the smooth expanse of her belly to the round curve of her hips and the little black leather bikini panties that concealed the treasure hidden beneath.

Her body, the heat she generated, the cotton-candy scent of her... He suddenly wanted to take her somewhere private and help her through the rest of the striptease, then discover exactly what treasures she had to offer. Did she taste as sweet as she smelled? Did she feel as incredible as she looked? Were her moves in bed as sexy as her moves in front of a crowd?

He stopped wondering when she looped the whip around his shoulders—all coherent thought stopped. Then she flashed him a positively wicked smile as she finished out the striptease with a maneuver that ended her dance on his lap with her breasts a few inches from his face.

On any other occasion, he might have felt a little weird to have half the people he knew see him in such a compromising position with a stranger, but tonight, he was feeling fine.

He had a vague memory of Max inviting the stripper to stay for the rest of the party, and at some point he ended up wearing her cape and dancing with her in front of everyone at the party. The alcohol must have been hitting him at its hardest during that time, because what little he could remember was a blur.

He was starting to come out of the stupor a bit when he glanced at his watch a little after 1:00 a.m., surprised at how late it was. The stripper was perched next to him on a bar stool, dressed in the tight little leather dress again, looking like his favorite Victoria's Secret model come to life—except for the Zorro mask she was still wearing.

He was pretty sure he'd asked her why she hadn't removed the mask, but damn if he could recall her response.

Judging from what he could see of her face, she was a knockout. Her hair, which fell past the middle of her back, had the sort of thick, silky texture that reminded him of the women in shampoo commercials, and her skin had a light olive tone that suggested possible Creole or Spanish roots.

She must have told him what her name was at some point, but he was too embarrassed to admit to her that he'd forgotten it. It was something literary, Shakespearean maybe, but what?

"Your brothers are kind of crazy, aren't they?" she asked as she watched Jake make a big display of drinking beer from the cup of a bra his wife Kelly had somehow removed without taking off her shirt.

"People say I'm the tame one."

She eyed him with interest. "You weren't acting very tame on the dance floor a little while ago."

Cole struggled to recall what he'd done, but no luck. He shrugged. "I'm just good at embarrassing myself."

"Well, at least you got that Jeannie girl to leave you alone."

He had? He couldn't even remember having talked to Jeannie Monroe, let alone having plotted to discourage her attention.

Cole's brother Max caught his eye, nodded at the stripper, and gave him the thumbs-up sign. Cole ignored him and turned his attention back to her.

"Maybe we should go someplace where we can actually hear ourselves think."

"Don't you like the party?"

He'd been loving the party since she'd arrived. "It's been fun, but I'm all partied out."

"It's only one o'clock. The night's still young." She smiled an intoxicating smile.

Okay, he supposed for a stripper, the night was just getting started around one. She leaned forward to adjust her boot, and he got a prime view of her lush cleavage. Suddenly, he was ready to stay and party all night if she wanted to.

Though he had other more intimate pursuits in mind. Crazy ideas, thoughts he shouldn't have been entertaining with a woman he didn't even know. But he was wild with desire for her, and with all his inhibitions stripped away, he could think of little else but taking her to bed and exploring every lush inch of her body.

The mask she wore, the leather dress, the boots… His thoughts were a jumble of black-leather-enhanced erotic images. Making love to a woman whose face he couldn't see had never been a fantasy of his, but suddenly, he was possessed with the idea—and equally possessed with the need to see her face. Since the second option seemed the safer of the two, he pursued it.

"You don't have to keep wearing that mask, you know."

A devilish smile spread across her lips. "But wouldn't you like to spend tomorrow wondering, 'Who was that masked woman?'"

"I always wanted Zorro to take his mask off," he said.

"I bet you're the kind of person who wants to know how all the magic tricks are done, too."

"Doesn't everyone?"

"The mask is staying. I don't want to ruin my air of mystery," she said with a hint of sarcasm, leading him to suspect there was more to her than a hot body and a pretty face.

He was more intrigued than ever, and he wanted to kiss her. He really, really wanted to kiss her. Did he dare?

He glanced around the room to see exactly how m of an audience he had, and for the first time he noti the crowd had grown thin. The only stragglers loc be people who'd drunk too much and weren't e equipped to leave. Cole realized that must have been his brothers had gotten a hotel suite instead of using Max's restaurant for the party.

"I guess the party's winding down. Would you like to walk somewhere for coffee?"

She sighed. "I really should get to work."

She started to move from the bar stool, but Cole stilled her with a hand on her thigh. "Don't tell me you have another job tonight."

The thought of her leaving was enough to ruin his birthday, even if it had technically ended at midnight. To hell with coffee—he had to do something to keep her here.

"I just need to help—" she started to say, but he gave in to the impulse to lean over and kiss her, ending her explanation.

If ever there was a good reason to overcome one's inhibitions with alcohol, the way she kissed was it. He probably wouldn't have kissed her so quickly under normal circumstances, but he was damn glad he did. Cole barely repressed a groan of pleasure when she snaked her arm around his neck and coaxed his tongue into an erotic dance of its own. If they'd already kissed tonight, he was sure that he would have remembered it.

Some details of the party might have been fuzzy in his memory, but the feel of his birthday surprise's too-soft lips, the taste of her, the tempting boldness of her tongue—those details were impossible to forget.

He wanted her so badly he could hardly breathe. Wanted to touch, explore, taste… He wanted their bodies tangled together until morning.

She broke the kiss and trailed her tongue along his jaw to his ear, her breath tickling his skin along the way. "You have a room here at the hotel for tonight, right?"

Cole, his ability to speak somewhat hindered, managed a nod.

"Then let's go."

2

The League of Scandalous Women's Guiding Principle 2:
A scandalous woman boldly enjoys her sensuality.
She does not hide it or feel embarrassed by it.
She uses it as a weapon only when necessary.

JULIET DIDN'T NORMALLY GO for one-night stands, but difficult circumstances called for extreme measures. Cole was exactly the kind of laid-back party guy she needed for a commitment-free fling.

He was even sexier in person than he'd been in the photos, and giving him a striptease was an even bigger turn-on than she'd thought it would be. It wasn't hard to tell he'd loved it, too.

"This is my room," he said, stopping in front of room 207 and peering at his key card, then up at the door number, as if confirming the fact for himself. That was her first hint that maybe he'd been hitting the bottle a little harder than she'd first suspected.

"How much have you drunk tonight?"

He flashed an impossibly sexy smile. "A little here and there. Not enough to cloud my judgment about this," he said, nodding at the door.

This, as in, spending the night with her. Butterflies fluttered in her stomach as reality set in. She'd gotten her sexy birthday boy right where she wanted him, and now she was about to have one incredibly hot, reckless night in his arms. This was what she wanted, wasn't it?

Yes, definitely. She did need a shake-up, after all, a reminder that she was still young and single and living the carefree life she wanted. But normally with guys, she was more careful than she was being tonight. There were too many creeps out there to take the kind of risk she was taking now—assuming she knew Cole well enough through his photos and memorabilia to trust that he was safe.

She usually didn't give it up for just anyone. She had standards, and she knew the club scene where she hung out was full of sleazebags. So it was natural to feel a little nervous about the chance she was taking tonight, but she needed it. She needed him. Right here, right now.

She had a set of rules for successful no-strings-attached affairs, and she'd be breaking one of the most important ones tonight—never sleep with him until you know his dating history and his mental state. But Cole felt so safe, so right, and if ever there was an occasion for rule-breaking, this was it.

Juliet's insides heated up as he pulled her against him and kissed her senseless. She'd intended to remove her mask now that they were away from Cole's brothers, to whom she'd have had to explain why their party planner, and not a professional stripper, had performed tonight, but now the idea of making love to a man who couldn't see her face was a definite thrill.

She broke the kiss and whispered, ''How about if I leave the mask on?''

''I want to see you,'' he said, his breath tickling her neck.

Then he took her earlobe into his mouth and sucked gently until her skin turned to gooseflesh.

The sensation sent chills through her. She suppressed a wave of shivers. "Isn't the mystery kind of exciting?"

He looked at her then, a half smile playing on his lips. "Yeah, it is. I guess you can leave it on for now. But I want to see you, eventually."

He'd get to see her—every inch. He didn't have to worry about that. But the thought of having anonymous sex, of him possibly never seeing her face, had its own appeal. Maybe she'd slip out of the room before dawn, leaving him to wonder about her identity. Or maybe not, but she loved having the option.

Once inside the room, he switched on a lamp, and Juliet approached him from behind and slid her hands up the back of his shirt.

His flesh was firm and hot, the muscles of his back rippling at her touch. She slid her hands around his torso and along the ridges of his belly until she found his belt. No sense in wasting time. She unfastened it.

He let his head fall back as she made quick work of his zipper and slid her hands inside his boxers. He was hard already, straining against her touch. She found his head and massaged it gently, then ran her fingers down the length of him.

His breathing grew shallow, and he reached down to still her hand. He turned to her and lifted her by the waist onto the bed, then climbed on top of her like a predatory animal.

Juliet emitted a low purr in her throat. He was exactly the kind of lover she liked best—hot and in charge. And when he pinned her to the bed and consumed her with a hungry kiss, she wrapped her arms and legs around him, clung to him as if he were her life preserver.

He pulled back and kissed her softly one more time. "You're sure you want to be here?"

She smiled, thinking there was no place else she'd rather be, and rubbed the back of his thigh with her foot. "Don't I feel sure?"

"Mmm." He slid his thumb along her jaw, then down the side of her neck to her collarbone. He dipped his head and kissed her there. "You feel like heaven."

"I've got protection, if that's what you're worried about," she said.

He licked her lower lip and ground his hips into her. "Do I look worried?"

No, definitely not worried.

She sighed and then ended their conversation with a kiss, long, slow and deep, one she could feel all the way to her toes. It made the unbalanced feeling that had been plaguing her since Rebecca's call disappear, and when Cole's hand dipped beneath her dress and found her nipple, she had trouble remembering what she'd been upset about in the first place.

All was right in Juliet's world.

This was the wild, uninhibited release she'd been looking for. This man, right now, was what she needed, just for tonight. She'd leave his bed a woman refreshed, recharged, reaffirmed. She'd leave confident again that the party hadn't ended, and a guy like Cole would totally understand. He'd be happy there were no strings attached.

When he trailed his tongue down the side of her neck and then pushed down her dress to take her breast in his mouth, Juliet arched her back and made a feline sound.

Moments later he'd made quick work of the zipper on her dress, and she was shimmying out of her panties. He unsnapped her bra, then cupped her breasts in his hands and tasted each one again.

Juliet stretched her arms over her head, closed her eyes, ground her hips against him. This was what she loved—the carefree thrill, the night of endless possibilities, the rush of excitement. As Cole slid his hand down her belly and dipped his fingers inside her, she felt relieved to know that her party hadn't ended.

"I want you now," he whispered, just as he plunged one finger deeper inside her.

"You've got me," she whispered back, and his second finger entered her, creating a sweet stretching sensation.

Then the third finger, and she closed her eyes to savor the pleasure, until she could take it no more and squirmed away.

He rose up and took off his shoes. Juliet helped him out of his jeans, then freed him of his underwear and finally his shirt. When he was kneeling on the bed naked, she sat back on her heels to admire him.

He had the sort of glorious body that deserved its own centerfold, all sculpted muscle and well-proportioned limbs, but she could hardly tear her eyes away from his face. She couldn't explain it, the connection between them at that moment. She felt tied to him right down to her soul, but she reminded herself that he was the one-night stand she'd just done a striptease for, and the crazy moment passed.

She was here to have fun, nothing more.

So she grabbed the whip from her costume that had been discarded at the foot of the bed and looped it behind Cole's neck, tugging him toward her. Not that he needed much coaxing.

He smiled at her not-so-subtle urging as he closed the distance between them, and then he was on top of her again, his flesh warming her wherever skin met skin.

Not just warming her—setting her on fire.

"Your striptease was amazing," he said as he took the whip from her hand and tossed it aside. "You've got great moves."

"Glad you liked it," Juliet whispered right before silencing him with another kiss. "I've got some other great moves, too."

She didn't want to discuss her profession with him any more than necessary. The less he knew, the greater the thrill, and Juliet was all about thrills tonight.

He withdrew himself from her momentarily and returned with a condom, which she took from him. She pushed him onto his back and removed the package, then placed the condom between her lips and put her mouth against the head of his cock. She rolled the sheath onto him, but before she could have any more fun, he pushed her onto her back again and reclaimed his position on top.

"That was a nice trick," he whispered.

"I know more fun tricks," she said, and then he shifted his hips and took her breath away.

He entered her slowly, his gaze locked on her, curious and intense. Juliet closed her eyes and savored the sensation of being opened up and explored. The delicious feel of him, all the way inside her now, caused her hips to squirm. She didn't want slow and sensual right now—she wanted hot and intense.

"I don't want to make love," she whispered, "I want to have hot, nasty sex."

He didn't speak, but the desire in his eyes said what she wanted to hear.

She kissed him with the same intensity she wanted him to return, and he got the message. He began to move inside her faster and faster, his body tensed all over as she locked her legs around his hips and matched his every thrust.

The fact that she could walk away from him tonight, her mask still on, and he'd never know who she was only heightened her excitement.

Their bodies worked toward climax at such a frenzied pace that she was nearly there before she could stop herself. She felt herself near the edge and she was barely able to will herself to slow down a bit and savor the sensation.

But then he stopped for her. She growled in frustration.

His body perfectly still, against her and inside her, he said, "Take off the mask."

She squirmed her hips. "Let's finish what we started."

A bead of sweat traveled down his temple, and she licked it off.

"After you take off the mask."

"What if I don't? Are you going to punish me?"

"No climax for you until I see your face. I want to watch you come."

"That's cruel," she said.

But also sexy. Really sexy.

"I'll hold you down and take it off for you if you don't."

"If your timing weren't so lousy, that might be fun."

"So take it off."

She was still so aroused, so tense, so close to the edge,

she had no choice but to reach up and slide the mask off her face.

He studied her, his expression a mix of appreciation and desire. "That's better." And then he dipped his head down and kissed her, long and slow. Afterward he whispered, "You're beautiful."

She smiled and tightened her legs around his hips. "Shut up and finish what you started, okay?"

"Yes ma'am."

When he began to move inside her, she tensed all over again. The delicious pressure built until it all came bursting forth in a rush she couldn't control. Her body contracted around him, drank him in, and then his own release came on the heels of hers.

Cole closed his eyes and moaned deep in his throat as he came, a light sheen of sweat dampening his skin, reminding Juliet of just how long it had been since she'd had such an intense encounter. He held her tight and convulsed against her, until they were both still, and then he kissed her with the passion of a man who'd thoroughly enjoyed himself.

She gasped for air between their frantic kisses, and when a pang of some unwelcome emotion—regret?—threatened to spoil her good time, she tried to push it aside and savor the moment.

This was what she wanted. Great sex. Meaningless fun. A commitment-free affair. So what if lying in bed with a stranger tonight left her feeling a little hollow? It was just a momentary lapse, a giving-in to the weakness of believing the popular notion that a woman had to be in a committed relationship to be happy.

Juliet would have none of that. She *wanted* none of that, right?

Absolutely.

COLE AWOKE to a hammer pounding on his head. He grimaced at the morning light and tried to swallow but discovered that someone had drained him of saliva and replaced it with a vile-tasting paste. With his tongue stuck to the roof of his mouth, he rolled over to discover a woman beside him.

Long, delicate arm, perfectly kissable shoulder, smooth, creamy expanse of back, chestnut hair draped over the pillow.

Who was she? And what was she doing in bed with him?

He peered around the room and realized he wasn't in his own house. It looked to be some sort of hotel room, and then he spotted a black mask dangling from a lampshade on the dresser, and memories started breaking through the haze in his brain.

The party, the whiskey, the stripper…the wild, sweaty sex with the stripper.

Oh, hell.

Cole looked over at the woman in his bed again and tried to remember if he even knew her name or her eye color or what she sounded like when she spoke.

He didn't sleep with strangers. He didn't go at it all night with strippers. Yet he had. No excuses, no blaming it on the alcohol, he'd done an incredibly stupid thing last night.

Juliet—that was her name. He breathed a half sigh of relief to have remembered that much, but then he realized he still didn't know her last name. Nor did he know her sexual history or anything else about her except for the fact that she stripped for a living.

And what sort of problems did she have that would drive her to take her clothes off for money? The moment the question formed in his head, he felt like an ass for thinking it. He, after all, was the one who'd dragged her to bed and done some pretty wild things with her based on her skill at taking her clothes off.

Cole tried to sit up but felt his head spin. Then the motion caused his stomach to rebel, and he nearly gagged.

Damn.

If his brothers could see him now, they'd be laughing their asses off. Their little brother—so bad at handling his alcohol he went wild with a stripper and woke up the next day feeling as if he'd been attacked by a construction crew.

He managed to get himself propped up on a couple of pillows, and the simultaneous spinning and pounding in his head settled to a gentle hammering. He tried to swallow again and realized he was in desperate need of fluids.

Across the room, a minibar refrigerator hummed quietly, but that might as well have been across the state of Louisiana for how interested he was in walking at the moment. He moved himself by sheer will to the side of the bed, then stood and made his way over to the small refrigerator, each step sending shock waves to his suffering brain.

Once he'd downed a cold bottle of water—and managed to keep it down—he began to feel slightly more human, and he sank onto the edge of the bed again, not quite sure if he wanted his companion to wake up.

But the movement caused her to stir. She rolled over and sighed, still half-asleep. He watched as she rubbed her eyes, willed his groin not to come to life at the sight of her breast peeking above the edge of the sheet as she stretched.

In the morning light, she was just as beautiful as he remembered, and it was easy to see why he'd been attracted to her. That, however, was little comfort for his stupidity.

She opened her eyes, and he was mesmerized all over again by their velvet brown softness. She had an almost startlingly pretty face, he'd discovered last night when he finally coaxed her to remove the mask. His methods may have been cruel, but they were effective.

She spotted him watching her and smiled. "Morning," she said, her voice gravelly from sleep.

"Good morning." Cole decided now wasn't the time for chitchat. She needed to understand he wasn't a one-night-stand kind of guy. She deserved, at the very least, that. "Listen, I'm sorry about last night. I don't normally—"

"No apologies." She smiled. "You didn't exactly force me up here."

"Yeah, but I didn't exactly get to know you first, either. I don't even know your last name."

"Emory, and yours is Matheson. Feel better now?"

"Actually, I feel like hell. I went a little overboard with the whiskey last night."

She pushed herself up in bed, seemingly oblivious to the fact that the sheet fell to her waist, providing a full view of her perfect breasts. When she noticed him staring, she smiled and settled back against the headboard.

Damn it if his body didn't betray him again. Even with the construction work going on in his skull, he still managed to get aroused.

Her gaze dropped to his lap and back up again to see his uncomfortable smile.

"I didn't realize you'd drunk so much."

He shrugged. "I downed a few too many shots before you arrived."

"Oh." She seemed to be processing the information. "I knew you'd been drinking, but your brothers told me you were kind of wild."

They'd told her that? He got a sick feeling in his gut that had nothing to do with his hangover. Had he walked right into some kind of paid services? Would his brothers really hire some woman to come on to him and sleep with him?

"Why did they tell you that?"

"Well, when they hired me, I needed to know a little about you to—"

"Hired you for what? To strip?"

She smiled, looking a little embarrassed for the first time. "Actually, no."

A jackhammer started working on his brain. He dropped his head into his hands and expelled a ragged sigh. "Please don't tell me you're a prostitute."

"A *what?* No!" She stood up from the bed, grabbed the hotel robe folded neatly on a chair nearby, and tugged it on. Glaring at him with a look of pure outrage, she said, "Hell, no!"

Okay, so he was a jerk in more ways than one. "I'm sorry. I just thought, when you said they hired you…"

"To plan your party! I'm a party planner."

"Oh. A party planner who strips?"

She sank onto the bed again, smiling sheepishly now. "Not exactly."

He decided not to push. She'd explain when she was ready, and he couldn't trust himself not to make any more stupid assumptions. "What do you mean about my brothers telling you I'm kind of wild?"

"I needed information about you to make the party personal."

"I thought that guy Finn organized the party."

"He's my assistant. I asked him to run things last night since I had other plans."

"Did my brothers hire you to strip for me?"

She shrugged, a mysterious smile playing on her lips. "They asked me to hire a stripper, but the stripper I hired came down with the flu, and when I saw your photos, I had a little brainstorm."

"You decided to strip for me yourself, based on some photos?" He wasn't sure whether to feel flattered or freaked out by the idea.

"Yes. But I did have some reasons that had nothing to do with you."

"Oh."

"No offense. I just needed to shake up my life a little, and I'd always had this fantasy about stripping for someone."

Again, his groin stirred. "You did a great job. I had no idea you were an amateur."

"I practiced on Finn."

Cole tried to form an image of her doing the Miss Zorro routine on the very obviously gay guy he'd seen flitting around the room taking care of party details last night, but nothing came.

She laughed at what must have been a perplexed look on his face. "It really helped that he's gay. He could give me objective feedback without getting aroused."

"That's an interesting fantasy."

She shrugged. "It was pretty fun, actually. Thanks for not being a creep about it."

The pounding in Cole's skull subsided enough for him to become aware that he was sitting naked in front of a near stranger. He glanced around for his jeans and spotted them on the floor next to the bed, but standing up too quickly sent a shock wave of pain to his head, and he grimaced as he sat back down again.

"How many shots of whiskey did you have, anyway?"

"I can't remember."

"Can you remember much about last night?"

He gave her a meaningful look. "I remember most everything that happened here with you. At least I think I do."

She smiled. "You're looking a little rough. Why don't we order some coffee and croissants from room service? Give you a little time to recover?"

Coffee sounded heavenly. Cole nodded, then groped his way back to the bed and stretched out on it again as Juliet placed a call to room service and ordered breakfast. When she finished, she sat down beside him.

"I'm getting the feeling your brothers lied to me about your being a party animal."

"They definitely lied. I hate parties."

"Oh."

He glanced over to see her frowning, her arms wrapped around her knees as she stared at her glossy red toenails.

"I mean, you threw an awesome party. Thank you for that, but I'm more of an intimate-gathering-of-friends kind of guy."

"Why did they lie?"

"That's their idea of a good joke. They think I need to

loosen up and sow all the wild oats they don't get to sow now that they're married."

She looked over at him, her gaze traveling from his belly to his eyes. "Guess you showed them, huh?"

"That's not why I slept with you, if that's what you're thinking."

Or was it? Maybe proving his brothers wrong had been a pleasant side effect, but it only took a glance at Juliet to know he'd slept with her for one reason alone—he was wildly, insanely attracted to her.

"Then why?"

"Because I wanted to. Because you're beautiful and desirable."

She smiled. "Thanks. You're not bad yourself."

"But I don't normally sleep with women I don't know, and I want to make sure you understand that whatever we started here last night, I'd like to explore it, see where it goes."

She stretched out beside him, her expression inscrutable. "I thought we were just having a little fun."

Cole blinked. Was he really having this conversation? He tried to think of an appropriate response, but his brain was being pounded by the construction crew again. He normally didn't go for purely sexual relationships, and if that's what Juliet was proposing, he wasn't sure whether he wanted to go along or if he even had the will to say no.

He knew no good could come of their having casual sex, and he should have been putting on the brakes, insisting they start behaving like mature adults.

She slid her hand across his belly, spreading her fingers wide, then moved it up to his chest. With that one simple touch, he felt a fire kindling inside of him, in spite of his hangover.

"Last night was incredible," she said. "I wouldn't mind a repeat performance sometime."

Sometime like now? Cole felt himself grow hard again as he remembered the way her body had felt, the way she'd made love with a complete lack of inhibition, with a sort of sensual enthusiasm he'd never encountered before. Suddenly, he couldn't remember why he was worried about behaving like a mature adult. Isn't this what mature adults did?

He couldn't muster a reply, so instead, he rolled over and wrapped his arms around her waist, then rolled onto his back again, pulling her on top of him. Her robe fell open, exposing her warm, perfect flesh to his, and she spread her legs, inviting him closer.

"I was thinking we'd have breakfast first," she whispered, before placing a kiss on his neck.

"That's probably a good idea." But his hands weren't cooperating. They found their way inside her robe and slid down the delicious slope of her back to her ass.

As he kneaded her flesh, his erection pressed between her legs, where she was already hot and wet, and he began to wonder what he'd been so freaked out about. Having sex with Juliet was as natural and easy as breathing. Not even his hangover was a deterrent from the pleasures her body offered.

"Really," she whispered and she traced the edge of his ear with her tongue. "We should get some food into you before we—"

A knock sounded on the door. "Room service," a male voice called from the hallway.

Cole felt an inexplicable loss as she extracted herself from him and tied the robe around her waist, then padded to the door. Or maybe the odd feeling in his gut was a sense of shame that his principles had been saved by room service.

Or maybe it was just the lingering effect of too much whiskey and not enough willpower.

3

___

The League of Scandalous Women's Guiding Principle 3:
A scandalous woman knows that victory in life's
battles is a reward for the bold.

JULIET SIPPED one last cup of coffee as she watched Cole eat with the hesitancy of a guy who had a killer hangover. She'd already put down three croissants and two cups of coffee. Great sex gave her a big appetite, and now she felt energized for another round.

But Cole, as willing as his flesh might be, didn't look quite up to the task. He'd responded enthusiastically enough, and she did want him, but the pallor in his cheeks wasn't going away as he picked at his croissant and sipped his coffee. Juliet wasn't a big drinker—she didn't need alcohol because she didn't have any inhibitions to lose—and she could tell Cole wasn't a drinker without his saying a word.

"You look like you could use a hot shower." She realized a moment too late how that might sound like an erotic invitation, when really she'd had the best of intentions.

A half smile appeared on his lips. "I'm not sure I could stand up for that long."

"You probably shouldn't drink, if it makes you feel this lousy and causes you to hop in bed with strange women."

"I think you're right, but don't worry, I'll be fine in a few hours."

"I just hate to see you suffering like this."

"Trust me, I've learned my lesson. No more liquoring up to survive a party."

"You really hate them that much?"

"I once climbed out a window to escape a college keg party."

Good thing Juliet hadn't been looking for anything more than a little diversion, because she and Cole certainly were no match made in heaven. One more reason she could feel okay about walking out the door today without looking back.

Except that there had been his talk of wanting to explore what there might be between them. Okay, so she'd been flattered by that—and a little freaked out. So long as the exploring he had in mind took place in bed, she was game.

Clearly though, they had little in common outside of bed, when Juliet lived to be the life of the party and Cole was Mr. Anti-Party.

He finished his cup of coffee and exhaled a ragged sigh, and Juliet had an idea—a quite brilliant one, if she had to say so herself.

"How about I help you with a bath?"

"I think I can manage."

Was this guy ever slow on the uptake. "You soak, I wash."

"You don't have to do that," he said, though she could tell he loved the idea by his halfhearted tone.

She flashed a wicked smile. "I'll get the water ready."

A few minutes later, hot water filled the bathroom with steam, and the tub was half-full. She'd found some scented bath oil in the hotel toiletry kit, and the damp air smelled of peppermint. Juliet went to the bathroom door and crooked her finger at Cole to invite him in.

She sat on the end of the tub and watched as he took off his jeans and stepped into the water. He had the body of an athlete, just as his photos had promised, and she knew from the photos also that his sports of choice were basketball and tennis. An unlikely combination that had provided him with a physique worthy of sculpture.

She felt her insides heat up as she admired the perfect flex of his buttock muscles when he prepared to settle into the water. After he eased down into it, he glanced up at her.

"There's enough room for two in here, you know."

"Believe me, I've noticed." She stood and shrugged off her robe, let it fall to the floor.

Then she brought a rolled-up towel to him and instructed him to lift his head. Once she'd arranged it, he leaned back and closed his eyes.

When she stepped into the opposite end of the tub and settled between his feet, he said, "Thank you," as if his brain still wasn't quite working up to speed.

"You relax, and I'll wash."

She took the soap and lathered it in her palms, then began to work it into his left foot. She kneaded and massaged, inching her way up to his thigh, and then she moved down to the other foot, paying careful attention to all the major muscles. There was nothing quite as delicious as a massage, and if the low moans coming from Cole's throat were any indicator, he agreed.

She skirted his groin area and slid her hands up his belly, straddling his hips as she made her way to his chest. As she pressed her fingertips into his pectoral muscles, searching for tension, she watched the contradictory play of relaxation and frustration on his face. When his hips squirmed and his erection strained against her, she knew which emotion was winning.

Juliet shifted her weight away from him and kept massaging. She couldn't help but smile when he growled and gave her a dark look.

She worked his shoulders, then turned her attention to his left arm. Desire swelled inside her, so she tried to force her thoughts to something benign as she coaxed the tension from his upper, then lower arm, and finally his hand. Paying taxes on her aunt's estate worked for about a minute, until she recalled the way Cole's fingers had brought such pleasure to her hours ago. Forcing her mind back to the details of the estate, she turned her attention to his other arm, and by the time she'd finished his right hand, she'd nearly succeeded in quelling her desire.

Nearly.

"Sit up and I'll work on your back," she said as she attempted to pull him up and move herself around behind him. But he grabbed her by the waist and pulled her against him, causing water to slosh from the tub and putting their mouths only inches apart.

"I want you," he whispered, and those three little words sent shock waves through her.

She wanted him, too, like she wanted air and water. He was suddenly a need so basic she couldn't imagine life without his body against her.

"Okay, but I have to finish this massage," she said, her strained voice a contrast to the wicked smile she managed to produce.

He narrowed his eyes at her. "You love to do things the hard way, don't you?"

"Mmm-hmm," she murmured as she ground her hips against him.

He said nothing, but he released her from his grasp and allowed her to sit behind him. Juliet spread her fingers across the plane of his lower back, stopping to pay extra attention wherever she found a knot of tension.

As she worked the tension out of his back, she began to wonder about this gorgeous man she was sharing a tub with. Other than the little information she'd gotten from his brothers, she knew nothing about Cole.

"Why don't you tell me about yourself," she asked, realizing too late that she was breaking rule number two for a successful one-night stand—learn as little as possible about the other person's life.

"Like what?" he said, his voice lazy as he relaxed into the massage.

"What do you do for a living?"

"I'm an organizational psychologist."

"Which means what? You organize the mentally disturbed into neat little rows?"

He smiled. "I help companies who are in transition or having problems in their organizations. I also teach part-time at Tulane."

Juliet tried to picture impossibly sexy Cole teaching a classroom of students, but instead she produced an image of him leaning against a desk, shirtless, as horny college girls fawned over him.

"That doesn't quite fit with my image of you."

"Why not?"

"I guess your brothers just didn't mention your work."

"My brothers haven't noticed that I've graduated from college yet."

Juliet worked her hands over his firm shoulders as she reconfigured her mental image of him from hunky party boy to bookish psychologist. She hated to think what he might make of her behavior last night and this morning. Masquerading as a stripper and hopping into bed with a stranger probably didn't suggest anything positive about her mental health.

"Are you one of those people who likes to analyze everything to death?"

"I've occasionally been accused of overanalyzing," he said with a rueful smile over his shoulder, "but I'll never admit to it."

"What will you admit?"

"That I took a bunch of psychology classes in college because I thought they were easy. I was a chemistry major well on my way to becoming a nerdy scientist when I realized I enjoyed psychology a lot more."

Juliet smiled. Maybe she and Cole weren't so different after all. "I was an accidental business major, myself. How did you end up getting your Ph.D.?"

"My guidance counselor told me the only thing I could do with a psychology degree was go to grad school."

"So you gave up your dream of becoming a nerdy scientist?"

"And became a nerdy psychologist instead."

"Nerdy is one of the last words I'd use to describe you."

"I've been called a little overly cerebral by my brothers. Get to know me and you'll probably agree."

Too bad she had no intention of getting to know him outside of bed. He seemed like an interesting guy.

She finished the massage, and when Cole turned to face her, she tried her best not to pounce on him. Rubbing him down had put all sorts of naughty ideas in her head.

"Listen, Juliet, last night was amazing—incredible—but having a chance to talk to you has reminded me of all the reasons we shouldn't go any further than we already have."

Huh? Had he decided she was too crazy to sleep with again? Before she could think of a response, he continued.

"Much as I want to, I know we shouldn't do this again," he said, glancing down at her naked body, "until we know each other better."

Yikes, this was decidedly *not* going the way she wanted.

"What's wrong?" she asked. "Do I have doggy breath? Do I snore?"

"None of the above. I'm sorry, I wasn't myself last night. I'd prefer to get to know you and see if we're compatible before we hop into bed."

"Except we've already hopped. And hopped, and hopped, and hopped." She tried not to smile at her own joke but failed.

"Yeah, the problem is you're unbelievably sexy, and I'm likely to lose all my willpower in about ten seconds."

"And you'd be violating your principles."

"You're making me sound like a real party killer. I just don't want either of us to do anything we might later regret."

Damn it. Principles were nice and all, but not when they ruined her fun.

Juliet suddenly felt ridiculous kneeling in the bathtub, buck naked. She started to climb out, but Cole stilled her with a hand on her hip.

"I'm sorry," he said. "This never should have happened, but I'd love for us to start out right, go on a date and get to know each other.''

Great. Just freaking great. First her aunt passes away and leaves behind a mess of an estate, then Rebecca gets engaged, and now *this?* She'd managed to find the one hot guy on earth who was morally opposed to no-strings-attached sex? Her temper flared, and she went from feeling ridiculous to pissed off.

''Thanks, but no thanks. I'm not interested in playing the dating game right now.'' She stood and stepped out of the tub, then grabbed a towel and stalked out of the bathroom naked and dripping wet, not sure why she was so angry.

Let him get a good look at what he'd be missing out on, she fumed. Really, she should have been happy. He was just making it easier for her to walk away, because if Juliet knew anything for sure, it was that she didn't want some commitment-happy guy tying her down—especially if the tying down wasn't part of a bondage scenario.

''Juliet, wait!'' She heard him getting out of the tub, and she hurried to towel off, then grabbed her dress from the floor. ''Don't just leave like this.''

She turned to him and forced a smile as she zipped up her dress. ''This was fun,'' she said, ''but don't feel obligated to be a stand-up guy and do right by me, or whatever you think you should do. I'm not looking for a commitment.''

''Don't you think you're overreacting a little?''

Was she? Maybe, but didn't she have the right to overreact a little when everything was going so wrong? Juliet answered his question with silence as she put on her boots, then grabbed her panties and purse from the floor. The nagging feeling in her gut didn't deserve any more attention than his question did.

Cole's expression darkened when she opened the door to step out, but since he was dripping wet and naked, he couldn't exactly pursue her. "Don't just walk out like this."

"Nice to meet you, and goodbye," she said, then closed the door and walked away.

4

_The League of Scandalous Women's Guiding Principle 4:
A scandalous woman thinks for herself. She
understands the value of her own ideas and
does not bow to popular opinion._

DELIA MATHESON HAD PICKED UP her last pair of men's
briefs from the floor. She'd ironed her last dress shirt, and
she'd cleaned Cheez Doodles out of the sofa after a football
game for the last time. If Max Matheson wanted a servant,
he could hire one, because she was officially on strike.

And as for their sex life, yeah, she'd miss that, but she
knew how to suffer for a cause.

Delia and Max had gotten married when they were both
twenty years old, and they'd had some rough spots. They'd
also had lots of smooth spots. But as they neared their
twenty-year anniversary, with each of them having turned
forty in the past year, they'd definitely hit a rough spot—
the biggest one of their marriage.

Delia glanced at her wristwatch and then looked around
at the state of chaos the house had been left in that morning
as the kids had gotten ready for school and Max had gotten
ready for work. Any minute now they'd all come home in
a flurry of dropped book bags and demands for something
to eat, and that's when the strike would really start to pinch

their lifestyles. The two older kids both had after-school activities—Brianna's soccer practice and Tyler's debate team—and Max was picking them up after work.

They'd all somehow gotten the notion over the years that Delia was their woman servant, and she was partly to blame for not putting her foot down sooner. She had insisted they all take part in keeping the house cleaned, but such diligence only lasted a week if she was lucky before they all slipped back into their old sloppy habits.

Her family assumed she had unlimited time to clean up their messes and take care of them. But between home-schooling their youngest, Katie, who had been lagging behind in public school, volunteering at the other kids' schools, keeping their household running and doing all the countless other "mom" tasks that were her responsibility by default, she rarely had a spare moment for herself. She was tired of all the thankless work, and she wasn't going to do it anymore.

Her fortieth birthday had passed by without ado, at her request, but she'd still felt disappointed that no one had thrown her a surprise party anyway. It would have both annoyed her and thrilled her, too, if such mixed emotions were possible.

The last straw had come a week ago, when Delia had gone out of her way to make a romantic dinner for herself and Max, even arranging for all the kids to be out of the house for the evening. She'd let Max know well ahead of time that she wanted him home Friday night for a special dinner, and she'd reminded him the day before, as well.

But what had happened when Friday night rolled around? Max had worked late and totally forgotten about her request that he come home. She'd spent the evening alone watching their favorite romantic comedy, hating every cute scene between the hero and heroine.

When she heard about another woman who'd gone on a marriage strike, she'd known what she needed to do, and her resolve had only been renewed at Cole's birthday party over the weekend.

Max had been so busy socializing, he'd ignored her all night. She'd gotten a little too tipsy and done perhaps a little too much dancing on top of the bar, but that was *after* she'd realized he wasn't going to pay any attention to her.

Oh well, at least some good had come of the evening— she'd been thrilled to see her overly serious brother-in-law Cole loosen up and have a good time for once. She smiled at the memory of him wearing a cape and dancing in a highly suggestive manner with the stripper. It was about time Cole did something wild.

Delia stepped over a pile of laundry Brianna had seen fit to carry into the utility room and dump on the floor even though the hamper was two feet away. When she heard the garage door opening, she made her way through the kitchen that was littered with breakfast dishes and into the living room cluttered with homework papers and computer game cartridges, then did something she hadn't done in weeks. She picked a book from the bookcase and sat down on the couch to read it.

The momentary silence before everyone came bursting into the house was almost too much. And she realized that in her never-ending pursuit of an orderly household, she'd nearly forgotten how to sit still.

Then the door from the garage swung open, and her family's chatter filled the house.

"What's for dinner?" Tyler called without bothering to say hello.

"Hey, babe," Max said as he placed his briefcase on the only empty spot on the kitchen counter, in spite of the fact that she'd asked him a million times not to.

"Mom," Brianna said in her I'm-about-to-complain voice, "Deanna Garrett said my pants are out of style. I'm not wearing these stupid things anymore."

Delia looked up from her book and cast a glance at the fifty-dollar jeans they'd bought only two weeks ago. She forced herself not to react.

"I'm starving, Mom!" Tyler stood staring into the refrigerator as if doing so would make food magically prepare itself.

How had she managed to devote her entire life to her family, giving up her own career to make sure they had a happy home life and a parent always nearby, and still have them turn out like this? She'd raised a bunch of cretins, and it made her want to run screaming from the house and never come back.

"Where's Katie?" Max asked.

"Having dinner at a friend's house."

He glanced around at the mess, then settled his gaze on the housecoat she was wearing. "You having a bad day today?"

"You might say that."

"What's for dinner?"

If she were a cartoon character, steam would have shot out of Delia's ears at that moment.

She forced herself to maintain her calm. "I don't know. Why don't you tell me?"

"Is this some kind of joke?"

Max hadn't cooked a meal in their entire marriage, and that used to be okay. He used to thank her for cooking, compliment the dinners she made, tell her what a great job she did of keeping up the house…

Lately, all her hard work was about as appreciated as the toilet. It went unnoticed until it stopped working.

"No joke. This is your official notice—I'm on strike."

Max flashed her a perplexed look, Brianna rolled her eyes, and Tyler began chugging milk straight from the carton.

"Mom's gone off the deep end," Brianna muttered as she stalked toward her bedroom.

Tyler stopped chugging to ask, "Does this mean we're not having dinner?"

"Um, babe, I hate to tell you this, but you're not part of a union. What do you mean you're on strike?"

Stay calm. No big explosions. "I mean," she began, her voice carefully even, "I'm not doing the mom job anymore. The pay is crap, and the benefits suck. If you want a maid, a cook and a personal assistant, you can hire one of each."

Tyler stared in awe from the kitchen.

Max donned his neutral uh-oh-she's-got-PMS face. "Maybe we should just order a pizza tonight," he said in the tone he always used when he was afraid she might hurl something at him.

"Pizza delivery menus are beside the phone book."

"I want Primo's," Tyler said, heading for the menus. He never missed an opportunity to eat pizza.

Max sat down on the couch beside Delia and gave her a concerned look. He was taking the strike surprisingly well, and she knew it was because he didn't really understand the repercussions. A few days of her not maintaining the household, and the whole place would descend into utter chaos.

"Maybe you ought to rest tonight, take it easy. You'll feel better tomorrow," he said.

"I'm sure I will, but I'll still be on strike."

"Did you see this on TV or something? I don't get it."

Okay, so she *had* gotten the idea from the woman on TV who'd made it on all the morning talk shows by going on strike against her family. But it was a good idea, and Delia wasn't doing this to get national attention. She just wanted her family's attention to the matter of their being a bunch of thankless slobs.

And now what? She hadn't really thought about what would happen after she'd declared her strike. With free time on her hands, she could actually do something fun. But it had been so long since she'd had free time, she couldn't think of anything fun she wanted to do. Clearly, no more reading was going to take place here in the living room with her hungry family stalking around waiting for pizza.

Maybe she could take her novel to…the bathtub. Yes! She could take a bath. She'd been pregnant with Katie the last time she'd actually read in the tub. She was long past due for a good soak.

"It doesn't matter where the idea came from," she said. "What matters is that you and the kids get the message that I don't appreciate being treated like your servant. When you all start doing your share and appreciating my work, I'll consider ending the strike."

"We do appreciate you."

She gave him a look that let him know exactly what she thought of his form of appreciation. "Now, you'll have to excuse me, because I'm going to take a bath, and I'll be locking the door. I don't want to hear anyone knock on it.''

Max's expression turned wary. "Okay, sure, sounds like you need some relaxation.''

Delia stood up and headed for the guest bathroom, where she could be sure not to find Max's *Sports Illustrated* magazines littering the floor and where no one would think to look for her.

From the kitchen, she could hear Tyler ask, "Is Mom going off the deep end, or what?''

"She just needs a break tonight, that's all,'' Max said.

Clearly, he didn't realize the seriousness of his predicament, and he probably wouldn't until he had to figure out how to work the washing machine on his own.

In the guest bedroom, she shrugged off her robe and left it in a pile on the floor for the first time she could remember. Then she stripped off her clothes and went into the bathroom to start a bath.

When it was ready, she eased down into the hot water and relaxed back against the tub. She took a few deep, cleansing breaths, and tried to produce a soothing image in her mind to focus on.

Maybe that Tahiti vacation she'd been dreaming of for years, or a trip to a spa, where she could be outrageously pampered.

But the images lasted no longer than a few seconds before they were crowded out by more urgent thoughts. What time was she supposed to pick up Katie at her friend's house? Had she remembered to bring the dry cleaning inside, or was it sitting in the trunk getting wrinkled? How much longer before those steaks in the refrigerator would go bad?

Stop! She wanted to scream, and then her family would have a real reason to believe she'd gone off the deep end.

This was how she went on strike? By continuing to worry about all the countless details she had to keep up with every day as a wife and mother? If so, she was hopeless.

Here she was trying to enjoy the first time she'd had in months to focus on herself, and she'd forgotten how to relax.

Delia had a lot of work to do, and it had nothing to do with the house or her husband or her kids. For once, she was going to take care of herself.

COLE GLANCED at his watch and estimated that the disgruntled employee he'd been listening to had about ten seconds left before he'd run out of air and would have to stop and take a breath.

Cole had spent the entire day listening to employees of Gideon Corporation vent about their merger issues. He'd been mediating the company's acquisition of a competitor for the past week, helping management develop strategies for smoothly integrating the two workforces, but today his mind wasn't on the task at hand.

All morning and afternoon—all week, actually—he'd thought of little but Juliet. He hadn't been comfortable with the way she'd left Sunday morning, and he'd been replaying events in his head ever since. He'd handled the situation badly, that was for sure, and he wanted to make up for it.

Maybe he should just leave bad enough alone, but he couldn't. She'd managed to intoxicate him even more than the whiskey he'd had too much of, and he couldn't get her out of his system. With memories of her heavenly body fresh in his mind, he couldn't manage to talk himself out of making contact with her again.

But he had a gut feeling it was more than her lingerie-model curves that had her on his mind constantly. He'd felt a connection with Juliet, a connection he knew was worth exploring. Never had a woman distracted him so much he couldn't focus on work or anything else in his day-to-day life, but she'd managed to do just that.

Cole nodded and mmm-hmmed at the employee, who still hadn't paused for air.

He had a feeling Juliet was driving in the fast lane, headed straight toward self-destruction. He'd seen it in his private life and in his professional life, and there were probably studies to prove it, too—casual sex was bad for everyone involved.

When the disgruntled employee finally finished venting, Cole wrapped up the meeting and was in his car driving before he realized he'd gone on autopilot. He'd become obsessed with the idea of contacting Juliet as he went through the motions of the commute home from work.

How would she react to seeing him? Would she have calmed down by now? Would she be willing to talk, to give them a second chance? He wanted them to start all over, go out on a real date, actually have a conversation fully clothed….

Not that he'd minded the undressed conversations. He just wished they hadn't occurred so damn quick.

There must have been a good reason he'd been carrying Juliet's whip, mask, hat and cape around in the trunk of his car all week. He'd been torn between mailing the stuff to her or hand delivering it.

And now, he knew the right thing to do would be to take

the things to her in person, because he'd never feel right about not seeing her again.

If Juliet couldn't see on her own that her behavior was unhealthy and that the chemistry between them deserved a little more time to develop before it exploded between the sheets, then he would try to convince her himself.

He dialed information on his cell phone and asked for the number and address of Any Occasion, the name his brother Max had given him for Juliet's party planning service.

Fifteen minutes later, he was looking for parking on the street near Juliet's business, his pulse racing at the thought of seeing her. Any Occasion occupied a dismal little building on the fringes of the French Quarter that probably hadn't even looked nice when it was first built decades ago, but Juliet had clearly done her best to make the business appealing with an inviting window display that advertised her services and a stylish handpainted wooden sign.

Cole entered the small office, and Juliet glanced up from her desk. She looked different in her professional attire, more subdued but no less sexy, and Cole realized this was the first time he'd seen her fully clothed in something besides a stripper costume.

Her expression instantly changed from pleasant to guarded.

"Oh, hi," she said.

"Hi. I hope you don't mind my stopping by."

"You're persistent, aren't you?" she said, closing a party supply catalog and pushing it aside.

At least she didn't hurl it at him. He'd take that as a good sign. "I've been told it's one of my virtues."

He placed the bag of Zorro accessories on her desk. She opened it and looked inside.

"Thanks for bringing these back. I couldn't think of a way to explain to the costume rental place that I'd lost them."

"You could have gotten in touch with me."

She suppressed a smile. "I can imagine that conversation— 'Hi, remember me? I'm the girl who stormed out of your hotel room and left my whip behind.'"

"Trust me, I wouldn't have needed any reminders about your identity."

"If you're looking to hire a stripper, I'll have to refer you elsewhere. That was a one-time service."

"Damn it." He produced a discouraged look. "I was hoping you'd perform for my grandfather's birthday."

She raised an eyebrow.

"I'm kidding. But seriously, I'd like to talk to you. If now isn't a good time—"

She made a dismissive gesture. "It's as good a time as any."

"So you'll talk to me?"

"Only because I feel kind of bad about last Sunday. I acted a little bitchy."

"Totally understandable given the circumstances."

She looked skeptical. "Is that what you'd tell one of your clients?"

He was about to point out that he didn't counsel people on personal romantic issues, but something stopped him. The study several students in his evening class were conducting popped into his head—how office romances affect organizations. It had nothing to do with the situation with

Juliet, and yet, something nagged at him. The idea of the study he'd been rolling over in his head earlier returned.

What if Juliet could help him do a little hypothetical research? What if he could use it to change her mind?

"Funny you ask that question," he said. "I have a theory about relationships, and you've gotten me thinking about it this week."

And I'd like you to be the subject of my own, private, one-on-one case study....

"What's your theory?" she asked, already on guard.

Yeah, what the hell was his theory? He'd better think of one fast, or he was going to look like a real ass.

Theories always made him think of Einstein—

"I call it the Theory of Sexual Relativity...."

Einstein, who was probably rolling over in his grave right now.

She looked amused. "Care to elaborate?"

"It goes like this.... Emotional health is relative to one's sexual practices. Sex without an emotional bond is always directly correlated to a decline in emotional health."

Hey, that didn't sound half bad for something he'd just pulled out of his ass.

Her smirk turned into a wry grin. "I'm impressed. Is that what you do all day? Sitting around thinking up theories about sex?"

"Sometimes I actually put my theories to the test."

He wasn't quite sure where this was going, but at least she hadn't laughed him out the door yet.

"Now I'm liking the sound of that. Can I volunteer to be your research subject? We can have casual sex and you can document its effects on me, eh?"

She'd said it, not him. And now that he had an opportunity to spend more time with her, convince her that he was right and she was wrong, he couldn't turn it down.

"I'd love to put the Theory of Sexual Relativity to the test, but it will require you to have an open mind about it. You can't just go into the study convinced that the theory is false."

The academic in him revolted against classifying any of this as a study, but the guy in him was willing to call it whatever the hell it took to keep Juliet around.

She crossed her arms over her chest, and the low-cut sweater she wore dipped to reveal her cleavage. Erotic images crowded his thoughts and erased the last of his reservations.

She smiled. "I think I can keep an open mind."

Cole felt an odd mix of relief and disgust at himself. "Great, so why don't we give ourselves, say, a month to complete our research?"

"One month," she said. "I get unlimited access to your bed, and you get unlimited chances to convince me your theory's not wacked? I can handle that."

Unlimited access to his bed? Cole was liking that condition a hell of a lot more than he should have. Yeah, he could handle it, too.

All in the name of research, of course.

5

JULIET WASN'T ONE to back down from a challenge, but she was a little surprised at her own bravado, considering the sick feeling in her gut. Cole's theory really didn't stand a chance, right? She'd never experienced any serious negative side effects of having sex without commitment, right? And couldn't she argue that the opposite was true—that people started getting hurt when emotions were involved?

Okay, so there had been a few bumps along the road, maybe even a near-disaster or two, but she'd been younger then, more prone to emotional entanglement. By now, she'd surely perfected the art of casual sex. And she'd prove it with Cole. No way was she just going to sit back and let him condemn her personal life.

She looked at Cole and remembered just why it was worth proving with him. He was damn sexy in his crisp blue Oxford and his summer wool pants that were cut to fit his waist and hips perfectly.

"I was just thinking—" he said.

"I'm beginning to suspect you do entirely too much of that," she said with a little smile.

His mouth twitched. "Maybe so, but would you consider having dinner with me tonight anyway?"

"You mean we can't just hop right into bed?"

He ignored her attitude. "My brother has a restaurant in the city, and he just changed the menu. I promised him I'd stop by and check it out. Want to come with me?"

"Which brother is this?"

"Max. He's the oldest one with the big mouth. Maybe you've heard of his restaurant, Blue Bayou?"

"Of course I have." In the vast sea of New Orleans restaurants, it actually managed to stand out as a good one. "I've been there a few times—it's a great place. I had no idea Max was the owner."

"So what do you say? I'll pick you up around seven?"

Juliet wasn't sure why agreeing to dinner with Cole made her feel much more nervous than agreeing to sleep with him had. She decided it had to be his interest in her as a research subject.

She nodded. "Sounds good."

He glanced at his watch. "I have a meeting to go to, so I'll call you later for directions to your place."

The front door opened, and her assistant, Finn Connelly, stepped inside, his arms loaded with shopping bags. His perfectly coiffed dark brown hair reminded Juliet that he'd spent his lunch hour getting a new haircut, and his meticulously stylish outfit reminded her that he had a crush on his hairstylist. "Hey Finn, you remember Cole Matheson from Saturday night?"

His expression transformed into a picture of smug knowingness. He'd spent the entire week casting sidelong glances at Juliet, clearly waiting for her to spill the beans about what had happened after the party Saturday night. But he'd known not to press her, and Juliet hadn't been sure why she'd held out on him. He always found out the truth eventually.

"Of course." He extended a hand to Cole.

After shaking hands, Cole said his goodbyes and left, leaving Juliet alone with Finn and his expectant gaze.

"Okay, okay," she said, finally giving in. "I know you're dying to hear what happened."

Finn feigned disinterest by removing baby shower supplies from the bags he'd carried in and placing them on her desk. "Aren't these teddy bear decorations darling?"

"Oh, okay. You don't want to know." She picked up a fuzzy brown bear and examined it. "The baby's supposed to be a girl, so we should stick some flowers or something on the bears' heads."

"I'm way ahead of you, my dear." He produced a bundle of pink and lavender silk and wire flowers from a bag, and twisted one into a little headpiece for a bear.

"So did Mr. Hunk of Burnin' Love stop by here to enlist your clothing removal services again?" he said, as coy as could be.

Finn didn't like to appear nosy. He considered it beneath him, although he was by far the nosiest person she knew.

"Not exactly." Juliet could play coy, too.

She loved watching Finn squirm. When she began making headpieces for all the bears, pretending to be completely engrossed in the process, he finally gave in.

"Okay, damn it. If you don't tell me what's going on between you and that gorgeous male specimen, I'm going to dress all these cute little bears up in red lace negligees for your friend's shower.''

She smiled, imagining how Audrey would react to lingerie-clad bears. The old party-girl Audrey would have loved it, but the new baby-obsessed Audrey might have a conniption. Juliet pushed aside the little pang of sadness that always came with being reminded that her party crowd had disappeared.

"If I told you what's going on between Cole and I, you might not believe it.''

Finn's eyes widened, and he pulled up a chair across from her. "Ooh, sounds juicy!''

"I'll tell you everything…'' Well, maybe not *everything*. "If you promise to take me out dancing soon.''

"Deal.''

"Cole is a psychology professor, believe it or not, and he's also apparently the last guy on earth still morally opposed to a little no-strings-attached fun.''

Finn rolled his eyes. "One of those—I dated a guy like that once. He wanted to fly to Hawaii and get married. I wanted to fly to Cancun and get laid. It didn't last long.''

At least Juliet had one friend left in the world who understood her distaste for commitment.

"Let's just say that Saturday night, he was more than a little alcohol-impaired, and he did things with me he claims wouldn't have happened otherwise.''

Finn smiled. "Naughty things?''

"Very naughty. And now he wants to make it up to me.''

"By doing more naughty things, I hope.''

"That's the problem. He feels obligated to show me the validity of his—'' she assumed her best anal-retentive professor voice ''—theory of sexual relativity, which demonstrates the negative impact of casual sex on emotional health.''

''Ooh, do I have some stories he'd love to hear.''

''He wants to do the getting-to-know-each-other thing.''

''And so what's the problem?''

''The *problem?* Would you want someone doing a study on you trying to prove how messed up you are in the head,'' Juliet said, conveniently leaving out the fact that she had volunteered to be his ''research'' subject.

''Sweetie, I don't need a study to prove that.''

''The problem is, he's really hot. And in bed, he's really, really hot. I can't just say no to further opportunities to repeat what happened Saturday night.''

Finn raised an eyebrow. ''But he was drunk as a skunk that night. Maybe he's a bore when he's not operating under the influence.''

''Exactly! And then my problem will be solved. I can tell him to get lost, and he'll have proof for his theory that I'm an emotionally damaged person.''

Finn was busy decorating a bear, and when he'd finished, he placed it on the desk. ''It's never that easy, you know.''

''Of course it will be. What could go wrong?''

''For one, you could really fall for this guy.''

Juliet laughed, but something about his concern bugged her. Cole was, after all, a hot guy, and what little time she'd spent talking to him, she'd found him to be interesting and funny, as well.

''Not likely. Get this—he hates parties. I mean, could there be a worse match out there for me than a guy who hates parties?''

Finn looked unconvinced. ''Cliché as it may sound, opposites do attract. I think you could use someone calm and professorly to balance out all your crazy energy.''

"Whatever. I don't have to worry about falling for him, because I'm not interested in a serious relationship. Simple as that."

She was a scandalous woman, walking the path of all the brave, scandalous women who came before her. It was a family tradition, after all, and she wouldn't deny the life she really wanted for the one society kept trying to tell her she wanted.

He shrugged and stood up from his chair, then gathered the flower-bedecked bears and put them back in the shopping bags. "You, my dear, are one deluded woman."

Deluded, maybe. But willing to give up the possibility of spending another night with Cole? Not a chance.

She was about to protest when the phone rang. Juliet answered and immediately recognized her landlord's Creole accent on the line.

"Miss Juliet, I'm just calling to let you know I've sold the building you're renting, and the new owner's gonna want you out of there."

Finn caught the look of shock on her face and mouthed "what?"

She ignored him, listening as her landlord explained the plans the new owner had to make the building a shop for tourists to buy voodoo trinkets, then copying down the facts as he gave them to her. She tried not to freak out, but the rising panic she felt suggested she was failing.

After she hung up the phone, she read what she'd written and blinked at the burning sensation in her eyes.

"What's the matter?" Finn asked again.

"This building has been sold, and we have to vacate by the end of the month."

"You're joking, right?"

"That was the landlord. It's no joke."

Finn came around the desk and pulled her up from her chair, then gave her a big hug. Juliet was not going to view this as a tragedy, just another setback in her setback-filled life.

Being forced to move with less than a month to find a new place to rent was far from the ideal situation, but there had to be a bright side. Maybe lightning would strike and she'd find the perfect business space—a location so perfect she'd start getting more clients than she could handle.

Or not.

"I guess we could operate the business out of my apartment for a while if we don't find anything by the end of the month."

Finn shook his head. "We'll find something—don't you worry. What about your aunt's house? I've been thinking what a great place that would be for parties."

"Except that it's in awful shape, and I don't have a clue how to fix up a house."

"I wish I wasn't tied up with school, or I'd help. I've always wanted to wear a sexy tool belt and go around drilling things."

Finn worked part-time for Juliet while he attended culinary school. He often provided the catering for the parties they planned, and the more he learned in school, the more in demand his catering services became.

"I'm sure you'd look fab in a tool belt, but you'll have to find your own home improvement project, because I'm selling the house. Would you mind going down to the corner and buying a newspaper? I need to start scanning the real estate ads.''

''No problem,'' Finn said, then disappeared out the front door.

Juliet glared at the lone teddy bear left on her desk, annoyed that she didn't have time to mope about her rental situation when she still had lots of work to do to get ready for the baby shower tomorrow. Not to mention her date with Cole, who presented her with an entirely different set of problems.

When it rained on her party, it really poured.

COLE PULLED UP to the curb in front of the imposing house Juliet had given him directions to over the phone. She'd asked him to pick her up here at her aunt's old house because she needed to take a look at it for something having to do with her business. The pale pink mansion had seen better days, but just looking at it was a glimpse back in history. He loved the old Garden District homes, and this one was in desperate need of someone to love and care for it.

He walked up the crumbling sidewalk to the front porch, then knocked, his body tensing in anticipation of seeing Juliet again.

When she opened the door, Cole was unprepared for how beautiful she would look. She'd changed out of her work clothes and now wore a red dress with tiny pink flowers on it, and a pink sweater draped over her shoulders. It was the first time he'd seen her looking so utterly feminine, so girlish, so irresistible. As sexy as Miss Zorro had been, Juliet's current look was far sexier.

''Hey, you look great.''

"You're not looking bad yourself."

"This is quite a place you've got here."

She shrugged. "It needs major work. I'm going to sell it as soon as I can find a good real estate agent."

Cole held back his urge to protest. It would be a shame to sell a family house like this one, but he figured he'd better reserve any comment until he'd gotten more of the story from her.

"I'm starving, so why don't we get going?"

"Sure. I'd love to take a look through the house later if you have time."

"Do you know anything about home improvement?"

Considering he had a minor obsession with fixing things, he knew some stuff. Cole's own house, built in the twenties, had needed work when he'd bought it a year ago, and he'd spent months doing home improvement projects on it. "It's sort of a hobby, actually."

"Then maybe you could offer me some advice about what to do with the place before I sell it."

"You'll probably get more advice from me than you'd ever want," he said, following her out the door. "We're only a few blocks from the restaurant if you want to walk."

She locked the door, then turned to him and smiled. "You read my mind."

Cole hadn't taken a walk through the Garden District in years, and doing so with Juliet was an unexpected treat. He savored the quiet, the scent of fall in the air, the crumbling beauty of the neighborhood.

"So you grew up here?"

"For as long as I can remember. This is where I lived until I left for college."

"And now?"

"I've got an apartment just outside the Quarter."

Cole had the urge to reach out and hold her hand as they walked, but he could tell from her disposition that she'd resist. Hopping into bed, she was all for, but he had a feeling more subtle forms of romance weren't her style.

"You seem a little stressed out. Something bothering you?" Cole asked when he noticed her marching straight ahead, her shoulders square.

"Sorry. It's been one of those days. I just found out I have to relocate my business. This, on top of handling my aunt's estate, is not my idea of a good time."

She explained that her building was being sold, and Cole puzzled over her problem, unsure why she didn't seem to see the obvious solution. He finally said, "Have you thought of moving the business into your aunt's house?"

"Finn already suggested that, but I don't think it's a good option."

"Why not?"

"You saw the place. It's a wreck."

"I'll bet it has good bones. It's probably just cosmetic stuff that needs fixing, and that's easy."

"Easy for *who?*"

"I could help."

She cast him a suspicious glance, probably suspecting this was all part of his evil plan. "That's too generous an offer. I couldn't accept."

"But I've already done everything I can do to my own place. You'd be doing me a favor giving me a new project to work on."

Cole wasn't sure why he felt so enthusiastic about the house, but the moment he'd seen it, he'd understood its potential. It was a diamond in the rough, and it deserved to be restored to its former beauty.

Juliet said nothing else. The expression she wore said the subject was closed in her mind. He decided not to point out how she'd be restoring her own family history, too. She didn't seem to be in the mood for lectures.

He would try again later.

They reached the main business drag where Max's restaurant was located, and as they strolled past funky little shops and antique stores, Cole realized the error in judgment he'd made deciding to bring Juliet to his brother's restaurant. Not only was he setting himself up for a million questions about her later—especially if they recognized her as the stripper from his party—but he'd also set them both up for lots of interested stares and inquiries during dinner.

He'd been so focused on checking out the new menu, he'd completely spaced out the inherent problems of showing up at Blue Bayou with Juliet on his arm.

Juliet stopped to peer through a store window at a display of a wooden cat-shaped clock, and Cole took the opportunity to admire her. A rare New Orleans breeze rustled the skirt of her dress, drawing his gaze down to her legs and her narrow ankles, one of which was accented by a thin gold anklet. As if everything else about her wasn't enough of a turn-on...

She turned and caught him staring. "You like it?"

She could have been wearing a rope around her ankle and he would have found it sexy. Cole forced an image of himself licking her ankle out of his head. "Yeah, I've got a weakness for ankle jewelry."

She smiled a sexy little smile. "I'll have to remember that."

Cole escorted her two more storefronts down to the restaurant entrance. Once inside, they were immediately greeted by Delia, Max's wife, who was standing at the hostess's counter talking to another woman. She didn't regularly work at the restaurant, but she filled in occasionally when someone else couldn't make it to work or business was heavy.

"Hey, Delia. You're working tonight?"

She smiled. "No, but I was hoping you'd make it by. I'm actually here having a girls' night out with an old friend."

Her gaze settled on Juliet, who smiled back and said hello.

"You look familiar," Delia said, apparently not making the connection between Juliet and the stripper at the party.

Juliet cast a split-second glance at Cole, and he realized introductions were in order. "Delia, this is Juliet Emory, my lovely date for the evening, and Juliet, this is my lovely sister-in-law, Delia Matheson."

The spark of interest in Delia's eyes said that she wanted to know more about his date, but she knew better than to pry now. She'd wait until later when she had him alone.

After they'd completed the obligatory chitchat, a hostess appeared and escorted them to a window table, then gave each of them a menu. "I can highly recommend the seafood bisque and the tilapia in crawfish sauce," she said, mentioning what must have been two new menu items.

When she was gone, Juliet cast a scandalous glance at Cole. "Guess your sister-in-law doesn't recognize me without my whip."

"You remember her from the party?"

"Wasn't she the one dancing on top of the bar at some point?"

"My memory's a little hazy about certain details of the party, but that sounds like Delia."

"Seems like you've got a fun family, for them to throw such a wild party for you."

"Fun is one word you could use for them." Meddlesome, loud, and annoying were a few others. "Delia's the best of the bunch. In fact, she reminds me a lot of you."

"Oh, yeah?"

"She's a party girl from way back. Before her and Max had kids, she had a legendary wild streak."

An odd look crossed Juliet's face, but he decided not to question it. "So she became a mom and settled down."

"Something like that. Though I've always suspected her wild streak is still lurking beneath the surface."

A waitress Cole didn't recognize arrived to take their drink order, and they simultaneously opened their menus when she walked away. After they'd decided what they wanted, the waitress arrived with drinks and took their dinner order.

When she was gone again, Delia reappeared, pulled a chair up to their table and flashed a conspiratorial smile at Juliet. "Girls' night out has been cut short by my friend's son running a fever at home."

"That's too bad," Juliet said. "Girl time is essential."

"You're telling me. This was my first girls' night out in years." She smiled. "But enough about me. If you need to know any dirt on Cole, I've got it all."

"Dirt? You mean he has a sordid past I should know about?" She grinned at Cole, who was pretty sure the worst dirt Delia had on him was that he'd sported some awful hairstyles in high school.

"You've got to watch out for Cole. His nice-guy act isn't an act at all. It's how he's snared countless women."

He might have dated his share of women, but he'd always been straightforward with them, and if that meant he was a nice guy, then he was.

Until now, he realized, looking across the table at Juliet. His little white lie about the Theory of Sexual Relativity nagged at him, but he'd yet to think of a way to make things right without ruining his chances with her.

Either he lied to Juliet now, and maybe some good would come of it later, or he told her the truth now, and she'd walk away in a heartbeat. It felt like a no-win situation. At least he did believe his made-up theory, even if it wasn't one that had existed before this afternoon.

"I'm sure he has," Juliet said. "He's certainly snared me."

Huh? Juliet was about as snared as a fox on the loose, as far as he could tell.

"No more flattery, please. I might start blushing," he said, and both women laughed.

"Where did you two meet?" Delia asked.

Cole and Juliet exchanged a look. How to explain? He didn't have to worry about it, because Juliet spoke up first. "We met dancing," she said, which was true, sort of.

Except Delia didn't buy it. "*Our* Cole, Mr. Serious, out dancing? His birthday party last weekend was the first time I've ever seen him…" Her voice trailed off as she put the stripper incident and Juliet together.

The table fell silent, and the only one who seemed to find the situation amusing was Juliet, who wore a smug little smile. Cole decided he could learn a thing or two from her happy-go-lucky attitude.

He smiled and said, "Juliet was the one in the mask and cape."

Delia's jaw dropped, and then she laughed. "I've always thought you could use a little wildness in your life."

"Hey, I'm wild," he said. "Sometimes."

Fully recovered from her shock, she turned to Juliet. "His idea of wild is not paying his taxes early."

Is that how his family really saw him? As a stiff, anal-retentive bore? He'd always considered his athletic challenges the place where he channeled his risk-taking. Mountain climbing, rappelling—weren't those activities risky?

He gave Delia a warning look. "Cut me a little slack, okay? I'm trying to impress the lady here."

"You know I'm teasing. I'm sure you haven't had any problems impressing her."

Juliet smiled at him, a mysterious, knowing smile that made him want to drag her away and make love to her.

Delia turned to Juliet. "So tell me, what's it like being an exotic dancer? I bet you've got some great stories."

"Only one," she said. "I'm afraid last weekend was my first and only performance."

"What do you mean?"

He could see Juliet trying to keep a straight face. "I was just, um, filling in for someone. My regular job is planning parties."

"Oh!" She made another connection. "You're the party planner Max and Paul hired?"

"Yep, they found me when I planned a party for Paul's best friend a few months ago."

Delia looked thoroughly impressed. "That must be a fun

job. What's the most interesting party you've ever thrown?''

Juliet launched into a story about a party for a group of Italian businessmen that went seriously awry, complete with trips to the emergency room and livestock on the loose. Delia listened and laughed until she had tears in her eyes. They seemed to have forgotten he was there, until Juliet looked at him and said, ''Cole's party has to have been my favorite though. I've always wanted to do a strip-tease for the right guy.''

Delia got the hint and stood up. ''I'll leave you two alone. I think I'm going to hit the mall before it closes, but I'd love to talk to you some more, Juliet. Maybe we could get together for coffee sometime.''

Juliet beamed. ''I'd love that, too.''

''The new menu looks great, by the way,'' Cole said, trying not to imagine what the two women might say about him when they were alone.

''Tell Max. He spent weeks agonizing over that thing.''

When they were alone again, she asked, ''Is all of your family that great?''

''I'm pretty lucky. Other than a few quirks, they're a good bunch.''

In the flickering candlelight from the table, Juliet looked more luminous than ever, and he realized she'd probably make a great addition to his big, loud, boisterous family. But then he remembered why they were really together— because he'd lied to her, because she'd volunteered for a month of no-strings-attached pseudoresearch sex with him—and he pushed aside the warm, fuzzy thoughts.

He'd be lucky if she was even willing to speak to him when she found out the truth. Which he should tell her right now. His conscience nagged at him to come clean, and he tried to think of the words he would say, the gentlest way to be honest.

Juliet, there is no Theory of Sexual Relativity. I just wanted to trick you into dating me.

If he told her now, she might forgive and forget. Or she might leave, and they'd never have a chance together.

Under the table, she slid her bare foot up his leg, then between his thighs. Her toes brushed his crotch, and he changed his mind about coming clean. He suddenly had an entirely different kind of coming in mind.

6

---

*The League of Scandalous Women's Guiding Principle 6:
A scandalous woman understands that her inhibitions
are the shackles placed upon her by society. She who
unlocks them is freed from the slavery of conformity.*

JULIET HAD BEEN OVERCOME with hunger pains during dinner that had nothing to do with food. Talking to Cole, having him just across the table from her, had given her every thought a sexual edge. She'd hardly been able to think of anything but what she wanted to do with him when she got him alone again.

As they walked back from dinner, he took her hand in his, and after a block he slid his arm around her waist and held her close. She'd welcomed the close contact. Her body had developed a delicious ache for him that only grew the longer she had to wait.

But when they arrived at Ophelia's house, he was clearly eager to tour it. She was curious enough about his perspective on renovations to set aside her desire for a few minutes, so she didn't attack him on the doorstep.

After all, she could get more money for the house if it was in better condition.

They stepped inside and the familiar old scent assaulted Juliet. She had gotten used to the idea of her aunt being gone, but whenever she smelled that odd combination of lavender-scented perfume mingled with clove cigarettes and dust, her heart grew heavy.

"So this is it," she said in a forced cheerful tone.

Cole wandered from the foyer into the formal parlor and looked around, and she tried to imagine the place from his perspective. Ophelia had always been scrupulously neat, but in her later years, as her faculties began to fail and her budget to hire a maid or a handyman dwindled to nothing, the house had become more and more dilapidated. Juliet had done what she could to stop by and clean up occasionally, but her aunt hadn't appreciated what she'd seen as a suggestion that she was incapable of taking care of herself.

"If you don't mind my asking, how did your aunt die?"

"It was a stroke, but before that she'd become debilitated by arthritis, which kept her from keeping the house up."

"How old was she?"

"She was seventy-four—older than my mother by fifteen years—but she had such a strong spirit I just imagined her living forever."

"She must have meant a lot to you."

Juliet nodded. "Ophelia raised me after my father died when I was three."

His smile disappeared, and his expression took on that concerned look people always got when they heard about her father. "I'm sorry about your dad. What about your mother?"

"She couldn't handle the stress of my father's death and her sudden single-parent status, so she left me at my aunt's house and disappeared. A few years later, she was killed in a car wreck."

Juliet disliked telling people about her family history, because it was a real mood killer, and because it caused people to needlessly feel sorry for her. She was totally over whatever sad feelings might have existed about her parents, but everyone found that hard to believe.

"That must have been awful for you."

"It happened a long time ago, and I was so young I didn't know what was going on. Besides, my aunt was always there for me."

Cole's gaze searched her, looking for any hint that she was putting up a front for his benefit. Juliet had grown accustomed to that, too. People just couldn't believe she wasn't permanently scarred by having lost her parents and being raised by her unorthodox aunt.

"Really," she said. "I'm okay."

He smiled. "I believe you, and I'd love to hear more about your aunt and this house."

His gaze settled on the grand mahogany cocktail table surrounded by high-backed chairs that was the focal point of the room.

"That's where the League of Scandalous Women usually met every month," she said. "I used to sneak out of bed to eavesdrop on their wild conversations."

"The league of *what?*"

"Scandalous women. Aunt Ophelia was quite the groundbreaker in her day. She formed a sort of club for women who defied convention."

"Must have been an interesting atmosphere to grow up in."

"It was." She could almost hear the psychologist wheels spinning in his head. He'd probably be able to explain away all her neuroses with the fact that she'd had an extremely unconventional upbringing.

Juliet followed Cole's gaze to a photo on the fireplace mantle. "That's my aunt, the late Ophelia Devereux."

He smiled. "She has an interesting spark in her eyes."

"She was a very unique woman."

"Like her niece."

"I couldn't hold a candle to Ophelia. She loved to raise eyebrows. The League of Scandalous Women was full of latter-day bad girls, and she was the wildest of all."

Cole laughed. "You're kidding, right?"

"Dead serious. I have some of her published work at my apartment. You can read it sometime if you're interested. She was a writer—a pretty controversial one."

"I'd like to read her work. Did she freak you out as a kid?"

"I didn't know anything different. While other women of her generation were being domestic, Ophelia was writing essays on sexual freedom and hanging out at coffeehouses. I tagged along with her and for a long time thought every kid's life was pretty much like mine."

"So that's where you get your unorthodox ideas about relationships," he said with a grin.

Juliet went to the delicate secretary desk that had sat in front of the picture window for as long as she could remember. She opened a drawer and removed her aunt's diary, which she'd finally started reading a few nights ago. She'd been surprised to see that it held no truly personal thoughts, but rather it seemed to have been a place where Ophelia recorded her ideas for her published writing.

The burgundy leather cover showed its age, and a gold latch that had once held the diary closed was broken. A few nights ago, Juliet had taken home the League of Scandalous Women's list of guiding principles to put on her desk where she could read it for inspiration, but Ophelia had recorded plenty in the journal itself that would give Cole a taste of her ideas. She opened it up and began to read the first page aloud.

"'Herein are recorded the thoughts and musings of Ophelia Claudette Devereux, a woman of independence and originality.'" She stopped and smiled at Cole. "She was nothing if not confident."

"She does sound a lot like you," Cole said.

Juliet shrugged. People always assumed she and her aunt were very much alike, but Juliet saw their differences more than their likenesses. Her aunt was her greatest role model, and while she'd tried to live up to Ophelia's high standards, she had a feeling she'd somehow fallen short.

"I think she was a little disappointed in me. She expected me to become the first woman president, or maybe a famous novelist. 'Party planner' just wasn't a grand enough aspiration in her eyes."

"But it's what you want to do?"

"It's my dream job. I built my business from nothing, and I'm proud of it regardless of what Ophelia thought."

"Good," Cole said. "You're lucky to be doing what you love. Not many people can say that."

Juliet turned her attention back to the diary, to the section she wanted to share with Cole. Ever since she'd read it earlier in the week, she'd been wanting to get someone else's reaction to it.

"Listen to this," she said. "'A woman's sexuality is her most powerful tool, and until she understands that, she is destined to be controlled by men.'"

Cole's eyebrows perked up. "Interesting."

"'After sexual power comes intelligence. An intelligent woman sharpens her mind at every opportunity and has an unquenchable thirst for knowledge.'"

"I think I like that better than the first piece of advice."

Juliet smiled. "So maybe I shouldn't admit that I was raised hearing stuff like this every day."

"I don't stand a chance against you then, do I?" he said, smiling.

She hadn't met a man yet who stood a chance against her. Men, her aunt had correctly taught her, were surprisingly simple creatures, easily understood, and often ruled by their desires. She was smart enough not to say that aloud though.

"With a Ph.D. in psychology, you can probably hold your own, don't you think?"

He smiled a slow, sensual smile that heated her from the inside out. "Did I hold my own Saturday night?"

"Oh, that's right—you can't remember, can you?" He'd more than held his own. He'd been the sort of wild, uninhibited lover she was willing to bet he couldn't be without the help of alcohol.

"I remember the important parts."

"Then you know you did."

"Have you read the entire diary?" he asked, neatly changing the subject.

"No, just the first few pages. I sort of want to take it slow and savor it, since it's one of the few links to her I have left." Other than this wreck of a house.

"Understandable," he said, then frowned. "You do still have her house."

What? Was he a mind reader, too? "I know, I know."

"Any chance this is the house I read about in college where the New Orleans art and literature scene was centered?"

Juliet nodded, smiling as she remembered the famous poet who'd always composed impromptu children's poetry for her. "This is it."

He looked at her like she'd lost her mind. "And you're considering selling this place?"

"Does it really sound that crazy?"

"This is your chance to restore a piece of New Orleans history, and a piece of your family history at the same time. You'd be crazy to give it up."

"I'd be crazy to think I can deal with owning a house this big and old. It's a money sinkhole."

Cole walked around the room, pausing to study photos and admire antiques. Ophelia had had exquisite taste and had never hesitated to buy things she loved. From the authentic Persian rugs on the floor to the eclectic mix of furniture, there were pieces of Ophelia everywhere. Being responsible for it all now gave Juliet the willies.

He turned back to her and studied her for a moment. "You could use the house for your business—get a loan and fix it up, then use it as an event center. You wouldn't have to rent out hotel space like you did for my birthday anymore."

"I don't know...."

"Why don't you at least keep an open mind until I've had a look around? Let me see what kind of shape the place is in."

Juliet shrugged. "If it makes you happy, I'll keep an open mind." It wouldn't hurt to see what he had to say after looking around.

"Let's take a little tour, then," he said, and Juliet led him through the parlor, into the foyer again.

They looked around the first floor, while Cole admired the crown moldings and the original architectural details in the house, commented on what he saw that needed fixing, and generally sounded more and more excited about the potential renovations with each room they looked at.

By the time they made it to the second floor, she had a feeling he'd offer to buy the house if she decided to sell it.

If? How had she gotten to "if"? Okay, so Cole's enthusiasm was contagious. As he talked about how easy it would be to restore the house to its former glory, she started feeling an unexpected twinge of excitement over the prospect.

She led him upstairs, and they entered the room where Juliet had spent her childhood. It was an odd mix of little-girl and teenager decor, dominated by an ornate antique cherry bed.

An old, familiar sense of longing filled her. This was the place where her dreams and aspirations had taken shape, where she'd spent countless hours staring out at her aunt's riotous jungle of a garden while imagining what her future would be.

Even back then, she'd dreamed of adventure, of faraway places and mysterious men—never of settling down and living everyone else's idea of a normal life.

Cole approached her from behind and placed a hand at the small of her back. "You're looking wistful."

"It always surprised me that my aunt never changed this room after I moved out. I guess because the house is so big, she didn't need it, but I thought she would have converted it to a lavish guest room or something."

"Maybe this was her way of hanging on to you."

Juliet laughed. "You didn't know Ophelia. She was the most unsentimental woman I've ever met."

"That doesn't mean she didn't miss you when you left."

She tried to imagine her aunt feeling lonely, and the image filled her with a sudden sadness. It had never occurred to her that Ophelia might not have wanted her to leave, but of course she would have been too proud to say so, in any case.

When Juliet looked at Cole, the sight of him, so much larger than life, so deliciously solid and masculine, erased all the negative feelings. She was here to enjoy the night with him, and that's what she would do.

Juliet went to the closet, where she reached up to a high shelf and pulled down an old shoebox she'd kept hidden there for as long as she could remember. "This is my treasure chest," she said as she placed the box on a desk and removed the lid.

Her prom photo stared up at her. Juliet, ten years younger, wearing a little sequin-covered slip of a dress that barely reached midthigh, standing next to a guy she'd only dated for a few months. Troy somebody-or-other. She could hardly remember him.

Cole picked up the photo and studied it. "You must have made a big impression on the boys at your high school."

"Probably, but I was pretty oblivious to them. I liked older men—artsy college guys who sat around reciting their own bad poetry."

"How about now?" He flashed her a half smile that nearly melted her panties.

"Now I'm a little more adventurous."

"Oh yeah? Any interest in overly analytical psychologists? I can recite bad poetry if pressed."

"Since you ask, I do happen to have developed a recent interest in psychologists. I met a really hot one last weekend."

"Really hot, huh?"

"I've got some of my own bad poetry right here in my treasure chest, if you'd like to recite it."

"Will it get me anywhere with you?"

She smiled and set the box aside, then closed the distance between them and slid her arms around his waist. "I'll let you in on a little secret. You can have your way with me anytime. No need to woo me first."

"I'm a lucky guy," he murmured, right before he kissed her, long and slow and deep. Just the way she liked it.

Her insides bubbled and swirled until she could hardly think of anything but Cole's naked body against her, inside her....

And then he broke the kiss.

"We'll never finish the tour at this rate."

"The house can wait. I can't." She ground her hips against his thigh, and he got the message.

"You're right. We can look at the house anytime."

"There's one more place I want to show you now though." She smiled. "My secret garden."

Juliet led Cole downstairs, outside into the backyard, and along the meandering garden path until they came to her favorite spot. The ancient gazebo was overgrown with bougainvillea and morning glory vines, and sitting underneath it at the crumbling stone table always made her feel as if she were in her own private little world, where elves whispered in the shadows and magic was real.

She sat down on the edge of the table and smiled up at Cole. "My aunt subscribed to the more-is-better gardening philosophy. This was a great place to play when I was a kid."

He looked around at the jungle of trees and plants lit up by the moon and the dim porch light on the back of the house. Everything was seriously overgrown since Ophelia had passed away. She may have lost her ability to keep things up indoors, but to her dying day she'd gone out to work in the garden, no matter how hard it had been for her. She'd called it her dirt therapy.

"I can see why you liked to play here."

"I still do," she said, patting the empty space next to her.

Cole sat down, and she leaned over to do what she was aching for. She placed a soft kiss on his lips, slid her hand up his thigh, and moved closer.

She knew Cole had been thinking of this, too. He'd spent an inordinate amount of time admiring her body when he thought she wasn't aware. Her outfit had been thrown together based on Finn's assertion that Cole looked like he might get turned on by the girl-next-door look, and Finn was rarely wrong when it came to men.

Juliet untangled herself from Cole long enough to shrug off her sweater. "It's a little warm out tonight," she said.

He'd have to have been dead not to feel the sexual tension crackling between them. They were destined to have a hot, memorable affair, the kind that she likened to fireworks—dazzling for a few moments, and then it was all done.

Easy as that.

Her insides reached their boiling point when he pulled

her onto his lap and pushed her dress up around her waist. She loved a guy that could take charge, and Cole hadn't disappointed yet. Now if he only proved to be as hot a lover as he'd been last Saturday night, she could look forward to a dazzling fireworks display tonight.

His erection pressed against her pink lace panties, and Juliet gasped at the sweet burning between her legs. She wanted him inside her so badly she could nearly taste it. She wanted him right here, right now, in the garden on the stone table.

Cole broke their kiss and whispered, "Maybe we should take this back to your place, or mine."

"I might have played little-girl games here before, but by the time I was leaving for college, I dreamed of playing big-girl games. Just like this." She paused to run her tongue along his lower lip. "Let me indulge my schoolgirl fantasy, okay?"

He may have considered protesting further, but she slipped her hand between them and gripped his erection through his pants. Expelling a ragged breath, he pulled her against him and kissed her like he meant it.

"You are one hot number," he whispered when they came up for air.

"Hot for you," she whispered back.

"I'm having a hard time caring if the neighbors see us."

"Don't worry, they won't. There's plenty of privacy here."

He kissed her neck, then found a tender spot and began to suck and nip with his teeth. Gooseflesh covered her skin.

"I want you to do that down lower, too," she whispered, feeling like a scandalous woman who knew how to ask for what she wanted.

Cole looked at her, his eyes clouded with desire. "How about here?" he asked as his thumb brushed her nipple.

She closed her eyes to savor the sweet sensations as he tugged her dress down, along with the lace cup of her strapless bra. He took her breast into his mouth and did just as she'd asked, gently sucking and biting one nipple, then the other.

She licked the shell of his ear and whispered, "I meant lower."

Cole gave her that look again, and then a lazy smile curved his lips. "My mistake."

He lifted her from his lap and set her on the table beside him, then stood up and removed his jacket and shirt, which he placed on the stone tabletop as a makeshift cushion from the cold, hard surface. Juliet sat on the clothing, and he urged her onto her back with a long, deep kiss that started on her mouth. Once he had eased her all the way back on the table, he slowly began to work his way downward.

When he reached her waist, he slid his fingers under the top of her panties and pulled them off, then moved his hands slowly back up her inner thighs, increasing the burning ache inside her with every moment he lingered over her.

He stopped at ground zero, then slid one of his fingers inside her. Juliet arched her back and sighed.

"Now we're getting somewhere," she said.

In response, he dipped his face down and did exactly as she'd asked, sucking on her most sensitive spot, nipping with his teeth until she squirmed. He continued to move his fingers inside her, first one, then two and then three, stretching her and pleasuring her nearly out of her mind.

He began a steady rhythm with his tongue that built the

tension inside her until she realized she was about to come, much quicker than she'd intended, but she was in no position to protest. Instead, she relaxed into the wave of pleasure and let it sweep her along until the delicious end came. Crying out, she bucked against him, squirmed, and finally grew still as the pleasure passed into contentment.

He kissed her clit one last time, then trailed kisses up her belly, over the folds of her dress still bunched around her waist, and over her breasts. When he made it to her neck, he said, "Is that where you meant?"

"Oh, yeah," she managed to say, still fuzzy-headed and spent.

"Good. I aim to please." He smiled as he cupped her breast and toyed with her nipple.

"Then you'll do more than just stand around smiling," she said. "I want you inside me."

"Like I said, I aim to please."

He withdrew his wallet and she took it from him and found a condom inside. As he unfastened his pants and pushed aside his boxers, she removed the wrapper. She slid it on him, and he slid inside her. She was slick and extra-wet from having just come, and their bodies fit together amazingly well—the perfect balance of hard and soft, large and small.

When he began to move inside her, Juliet watched pleasure play across his face. Their gazes locked, and she felt that soul-deep connection again. The feeling thrilled her and terrified her, and it made her look away. Whatever it was, it was too heavy for a fun, carefree fling, and that's all they were having.

She slid her fingers up his bare chest, teasing his flesh as he built momentum, as their bodies crashed together.

And then he leaned over her, resting on his arms as he dipped his head and muffled their moans with a kiss.

The sounds of evening in the garden harmonized with their lovemaking, and Juliet could think of no more appropriate background music than singing crickets and whispering trees. She felt Cole tense beneath her fingertips, noted the urgency of his pace, and knew he was close to coming.

So close.

She tightened herself around him, flexing her inner muscles until she, too, was ready to fall into bliss again. And then with little warning, she did, and her climax drove him over the edge with her.

He pushed deep inside one last time as he spilled himself into her, and he cupped her face with one hand as he kissed her desperately.

After a few moments, the frenzy had passed, and he stopped to look at her.

"Are you okay like this?" He shifted his weight off of her and onto the arm he was resting on.

"I'm feeling fine," she whispered.

He smiled. "I meant, is the table bothering you?"

"Table? What table?"

He kissed her again, this time a soft, slow kiss that warmed her to her toes.

When he looked at her again, he said, "Come home with me tonight."

Her body said yes, and her brain said uh-oh. This was a definite rule-breaker. She'd already made the mistake of spending the night with him once, and it had nearly ruined their fun. She wouldn't do it again. "If you've got in mind more of what we just did, I'm tempted...."

"But?"

"I think we should establish a few ground rules," she said in the lightest tone she could muster, not wanting to kill the mood.

"Like what? No spending the night?"

"It would help keep us from getting carried away."

"Isn't that one of the best parts of romance?"

He shifted away from her, and she sat up and pulled her bra and dress into place. Cole set about straightening himself back up, too, as she tried to think of the most diplomatic response. They clearly were looking for different things from this relationship.

Cole wanted to prove to her she was wrong, and she wanted to have great sex.

"It depends on what you want. I know we have different interests here."

His expression darkened, but instead of retreating as a lot of guys would have, he stood his ground, even wedged himself between her legs and slid his hands around her waist so that she had no choice but to sit there and look him in the eye.

"What are your interests?" he asked.

"I'm interested in us having sex. We're great in bed—and in the garden," she added with a smile, "and I just want to have a little fun. Rules exist to keep anyone from getting hurt and ruining the fun."

"What are the rules?" Cole asked, clearly not pleased with the idea.

Juliet thought of her own personal set of four ground rules and decided one of them no longer applied. Rule number one—never sleep with him until you know his sexual history and his mental state. Cole seemed safe.

"Let's make three rules. First, no spending the night. Second, we need to avoid getting to know each other any more than necessary."

"How can I test my theory if I don't get to know you?"

"How can I prove your theory wrong if we don't keep it casual?"

"You're muddying the water here."

"Third rule, stay focused on the sex. Now does that clear things up for you?"

"So what? I'm your sexual diversion?"

"Something like that," she said, hoping it would come out sounding as playful as she meant it.

"I don't see how we can complete our research if you aren't at least open to the possibility of something more."

"I don't see how we can conduct your so-called research at all unless you agree to those ground rules."

Surely she could prove herself right—but what if she couldn't? What if Cole was right, and her whole personal life was thrown off course by him?

Whatever. She couldn't live her life worrying about what-ifs.

"I'll accept the rules if you'll accept the possibility of something more than sex happening between us."

She could tell he wasn't going to give in, even if his rule nearly contradicted hers.

"Okay, I'll admit that anything's possible," she finally said. Like, she could grow wings, fly into outer space, and become the first president of Mars.

Juliet stood up from the table and tugged her sweater back on. She kissed Cole one more time, wanting the night to end on a positive note.

But the intimate contact caused desire to surge inside her

again, and suddenly she could hardly resist the urge to go home with him. Maybe it was a touch of hormonal insanity, maybe it had to do with the way Cole made her feel— whatever the case, it was wrongheaded and foolish.

"How about we finish the tour?" Cole said, and Juliet nodded, thankful for the distraction.

She showed him around the rest of the house, watching as he peered into closets, tested the sturdiness of walls and floors, poked around windows, and tried out the ancient bathroom fixtures. All the while, she couldn't stop wondering if he'd be game for another round of what they'd done in the garden, but he was so engrossed in checking out the house, she didn't have the heart to interrupt him. Finally, they ended up back on the front porch.

"So, what's your prognosis, Doctor?" she asked, half hoping he'd declare the place a lost cause.

"It looks like this house does have good bones. Have you had it inspected yet?"

"I haven't had time." Which was sort of true. But there was also the fact that some little niggling feeling had held her back, and she'd simply put the task off.

She saw now that maybe the finality of moving forward with selling the place scared her just as much as not selling it did.

"We need to do that, but it looks to me like a sound structure in need of mostly cosmetic work. The only big job I see is the roof, which needs replacing, judging by some stains on the upstairs ceiling."

We? Since when had this become a "we" project? Juliet should have bristled at his presumptuousness, but instead, she found it comforting to feel like someone else was in it with her.

"How much will all this cosmetic work and roof repair cost?"

His gaze turned skyward as he did math calculations in his head. "It depends on how well you want the house renovated. To do the bare minimum, maybe twenty thousand or so if we do a lot of the work ourselves."

"Twenty thousand for the *bare minimum?*"

Cole shrugged. "It's a rough estimate, but the cost of replacing the roof will be at least half of that, maybe more."

Instead of protesting, Juliet was surprised to hear herself say, "I'd need a loan—and I'd need to move out of my apartment and into the house to be able to cover any new loan payments."

"Good idea to keep those things in mind."

She imagined herself in work overalls ripping up old carpet, and she laughed. "I'm really not a do-it-yourself kind of girl."

He smiled. "You can learn. Painting's easy, and most everything else is tedious more than it is difficult."

"Are you really sure you want to get involved in such a big project?" she asked, feeling dangerously close to agreeing.

"Positive."

And then she imagined all sorts of interesting scenarios between her and Cole as they renovated the house. Sweaty, grungy, sexy scenarios…

Where had this crazy urge to keep the house come from? She'd possibly become intoxicated by the night air or the aftereffects of making love to Cole. Or maybe she was finally willing to face the fact that as much as she didn't want to be tied down by the house, she also didn't want to give it up.

"Okay," she said, feeling queasy. "Let's do it."

Cole beamed. "Great. I know a good inspector I can call tomorrow to schedule an inspection."

She locked up the house, and Cole walked her to her car parked on the street out front.

"When can I see you again?" he asked.

"I'm free tomorrow night, if you're in need of a research partner again."

He smiled. "I think we still have plenty of research to do. Tomorrow would be great."

"I'm throwing a baby shower in the afternoon, but I could meet you afterward."

"How about dinner at my place? Around six o'clock?"

"Sure, so long as we'll be doing more than just having dinner," she said, keeping with rule number three for a successful no-strings-attached affair—stay focused on the sex. No getting distracted by good company, good food or good conversation.

Yep, Juliet was a pro at this stuff. Funny though that for the first time in her adult life, she was finding it incredibly difficult to abide by her own rules.

7

The League of Scandalous Women's Guiding Principle 7:
A scandalous woman knows the difference between
lust and love, and she never confuses the two. She
understands the merits and inherent problems of each.

JULIET SPENT SATURDAY MORNING prepping for the shower, but as she double-checked supplies, picked up the cake from the bakery and set up the decorations in her apartment, she found herself unable to think baby shower thoughts.

For one thing, there were the erotic memories of last night in the garden that had been plaguing her. Her schoolgirl fantasies couldn't have begun to compare to the real thing with Cole, and she'd hardly been able to sleep, she wanted him in her bed so badly.

For another thing, there was the stress of having decided to keep the house. She'd lain awake second-guessing her decision all night—the only subject that successfully distracted her from erotic images of Cole.

She had a feeling she was just using Cole as a diversion from the stress in her life lately, and if that was the case—great. She couldn't think of a better stress reliever. But she had to be careful not to hurt Cole in the process. That was the tricky part.

Once she'd gotten her apartment looking like a baby shower wonderland—complete with flower-bedecked teddy bears and pastel balloons and streamers everywhere—Juliet headed out for her lunch date with Rebecca, remembering to grab a few wedding supply catalogs on her way out the door.

The restaurant where they were meeting was only a few blocks from Juliet's apartment, so she walked, taking advantage of the mild fall weather.

In the restaurant, Juliet spotted Rebecca sitting at a table for two beside the front window. She waved and took note of her friend's healthy glow that seemed to have nothing to do with the sun in Cancun. Her skin wasn't tanned so much as it was luminous, and if that's what engagement did for Rebecca, Juliet had a feeling she was going to have a hard time continuing to pout about it.

"You look like you've been having entirely too much fun," she said as she pulled out a funky black chair across the table from her friend.

Rebecca flashed a dazzling smile. "I can't wait for you to meet Alec—he's flying out from California to visit in two weeks." She produced an envelope from the table. "I brought photos!"

Juliet sank into the chair and glanced around at the restaurant, trying to ignore the sick feeling she got at the thought of seeing the guy who'd stolen her last single friend. Ruby Q's was a yuppified jazz club by night and a hip little bistro by day, and it was Juliet's favorite place to get a shrimp po' boy.

"Why don't we look at the photos after we order," she said, and Rebecca's expression transformed from a smile to her signature what's-the-deal look.

"What's going on with you, Jule? You sounded really weird on the phone last time we talked."

Juliet bit her lip and pretended to read the menu.

"And you know you want the shrimp po' boy, so why are you acting like you're interested in the menu?"

Damn it, she'd never been good at hiding her feelings from Rebecca. Juliet put down the menu and tried not to look too guilty.

"I'll admit, I'm a little shocked by your sudden engagement—"

"A little?"

"Okay, I'm blown away by it."

"I know it's really sudden, but I'm happy! Doesn't that make *you* happy?"

"Oh sure, make me feel like a toad."

"It's all about you, all the time—isn't that right?"

Rebecca had an uncanny knack for getting right to the heart of the matter.

"You said it, not me." Juliet tried not to smile and failed.

"Are you afraid I'm not going to have time to do girl stuff with you anymore?"

She shrugged. "Maybe a little."

"I'll always make time for you, so stop worrying."

"Really? What about Teresa, and Audrey, and Mona? They all said the same thing, and now I hear from them *maybe* at Christmas with one of those generic 'Dear Friends and Family' letters. I wouldn't even be in touch with Audrey lately if I wasn't hosting her shower."

Rebecca dismissed her concerns with a wave of her hand. "Oh, please. They all have kids now, and we're not planning on children for a while."

Children? Rebecca, Miss I-Don't-Do-Childbirth, had discussed *children?* This was getting way too weird.

Juliet realized too late that she was staring at her friend with her jaw sagging. So much for disguising her shock.

"I know, I know. I've said things in the past that might make you think I'd never want children. But—" she got a starry-eyed look as she seemed to let her thoughts drift "—I don't know, ever since I met Alec, I just can't stop imagining what our kids will look like."

Juliet knew then that she'd somehow entered a bizarro world where everything was the opposite of what she expected. "Wow, you're really serious about this guy."

Rebecca looked at Juliet as if she'd just started dancing on the table. "Yeah, I'd say marriage is a serious step."

"I'm sorry. I guess I just need a little time to adjust, that's all."

"I hope you don't need too much time, because we've got a wedding to plan," Rebecca said as she produced a stack of bridal magazines from her bag, which prompted Juliet to dig out her supply catalogs and add them to the stack.

A waiter arrived to take their order, and when he left, Juliet vowed to put her bratty feelings aside and do what she could to help.

"Before we talk wedding," Rebecca said, "tell me what's been going on with you."

Should she tell her? Juliet considered keeping the whole stripper weekend a secret, but Rebecca could always tell when she was hiding something.

"I did something a little crazy last Saturday, and now I'm in sort of a predicament."

"You did something crazy? Doesn't that happen on a daily basis?"

"Well, not quite this crazy." She explained the birthday party, the striptease, and then gave the highlights of her night with Cole.

When she finished, Rebecca simply stared at her, wide-eyed.

"Have I actually managed to shock you?"

"You *stripped* for this guy in front of an audience?"

"I know, it was a little crazy even for me."

"And so what's the problem?"

"The problem is, now he wants to go steady or something."

Rebecca laughed. "No kidding, you sleep with a guy and he has the nerve to want something more from you."

"Exactly," Juliet said, though she had the feeling she was being baited.

"So maybe you should do what he wants and see where it goes with him."

"But I don't want a serious relationship right now."

"I know, I know, you don't need a guy to be happy. But you never know—"

"Stop right there. Just because you're tying the knot, that doesn't mean I want to do the same thing."

"I know you don't think you do, but neither did I until I met Alec."

"Cole was supposed to be a one-night stand. Nothing more. Things have just gotten a little out of hand."

"Jule, what's really going on? I've never known you to go out looking for a one-nighter."

"You haven't seen Cole Matheson. He's really, really hot."

"So then why not keep him around for some repeat performances?"

"Well, I guess I am. He hasn't given me much choice."

And strangely, Juliet was having a hard time feeling trapped by Cole's proposal. Maybe he wanted more than she had in mind, but she'd never had a problem extracting herself from relationships in the past. No reason why this one should be any different.

"A hot guy wants to date you, and you've got a problem with that?"

"Not so long as he understands I'm not looking for happily ever after."

"But he is?"

"Apparently."

Rebecca got that dreamy look in her eyes again. "I think happily ever after has gotten a bad rap. You might want to give it a chance."

Juliet nearly spit out the tea she'd just taken a drink of. Her life had officially gotten too weird. "This from the girl who once broke up with a guy for daring to leave his toothbrush in your bathroom?"

"I'd like to think I've grown up since then."

"You mean since last month?"

Rebecca shot her the look of death. "Very funny. Meeting Alec has been a life-changing experience, and I'd thought as my best friend, you'd be happy for me."

"I am. Really. I'm sorry for the attitude."

"Jule, I'm a little worried about you. We're both twenty-nine years old—quickly closing in on thirty—and you can't possibly think that you'll find any kind of lasting happiness hanging out at nightclubs and doing the disposable date routine forever."

"Look at my aunt. Ophelia found her own happiness without falling for the conventional version of it."

Rebecca's expression turned sad. "I know she's your biggest role model, but did you ever stop to think that maybe she wasn't all that happy?"

"Of course she was, and you of all people should know that." Rebecca had spent many an afternoon talking to Ophelia, keeping her distracted while Juliet cleaned the house.

"I think she showed each of us different sides of herself. She didn't want you to think she was disappointed with her life, but when she talked to me, she seemed sad."

Juliet blinked at the sudden burning behind her eyelids. Her aunt had always been her model of strength, courage and creativity. She was the one woman Juliet had ever known who'd dared to live exactly as she pleased, societal conventions be damned. To think that she hadn't been happy... Juliet couldn't. It was unthinkable.

"I'm sorry. It must be a shock to hear that."

Juliet shook her head and plastered on a happy face. "No, it's okay. She might have been sad that she wasn't able to get around like she once could, but not about the way she'd lived her life."

Rebecca looked doubtful, but she didn't say anything more. Juliet decided a change of topic was far overdue, so she turned her attention to the wedding magazines and catalogs on the table.

Instant distraction.

After they'd flipped through the glossy photos of perfect brides in perfect dresses for a few minutes, their food arrived, and they ate while discussing what Rebecca wanted for her wedding. Juliet still couldn't shake the feeling that she'd entered a strange parallel universe, and the feeling only grew as they finished lunch and headed back to Juliet's apartment for the baby shower. But Rebecca was happy, and that counted for a lot. She just had to keep reminding herself of it.

An hour later, her apartment was filled with women bearing gifts concealed in cutesy wrapping paper, and bubbly conversation about stretch marks and pregnancy cravings filled the air. Many of these same women had been Juliet's fellow partyers a few years ago. Now they'd traded in their minidresses for suburban soccer mom attire, and instead of driving hip little single-girl cars, they almost invariably drove minivans.

Juliet still liked them as friends, but she couldn't help feeling as if they'd joined a cult, and she was the only one who'd managed not to get brainwashed. When she wasn't taking care of running the shower, she spent her time talking to the only other single woman at the party, who was easily identified by the bewildered look she got when the conversation turned to natural childbirth versus epidurals.

Someone mentioned using something called a birthing ball, and someone else started talking about natural oil massages to avoid an episiotomy, and Juliet's stomach did a flip-flop. She invited her single-girl companion into the kitchen to see how Finn was doing with the food.

They found him painstakingly placing little sprigs of mint on the tiny sandwiches he'd made.

"Need some help?" Juliet asked.

"I'd love some." He shoved a bowl of mint at her and then hurried over to the stove to take care of something that was boiling there.

"We've run away from the childbirth talk."

"Ah, the female version of the war story," Finn said as he stirred.

The woman whose name Juliet had managed to forget shivered. "Episiotomies alone are enough to make me think twice about having kids."

"Just think Kegels," Finn said over his shoulder. "Those marvelous little exercises will keep your man happy. And I've heard that if they have to snip you during childbirth, they can always do a nice little sewing job afterward to make things more fun for him, too."

"Um, Finn, how do you know this stuff?"

"I've got a sister, remember? The baby machine?"

"Oh, right." Finn's sister had three kids and was working on number four. "I just thought we could count on you to talk about something more interesting than childbirth."

"What could be more interesting? You girls are lucky you get to do the whole birth thing."

"Maybe we can figure out some way for you to do it for us, then."

He turned to her with his eyebrow quirked. "You know, I've always thought if you ever decide you want a kid, we could have one."

Juliet gripped the edge of the counter to steady herself in case she passed out. "What?"

"Well, since you *are* on the path to spinsterhood, it doesn't seem like you'll be having a family the traditional way, and I'd like to have a little Finn or Finnola Junior someday—"

"Finn, in case you've forgotten, you're gay, and I'm female."

He rolled his eyes. "Of course we wouldn't have *sex*. We could do the artificial insemination thing."

Juliet stared at him, speechless.

"It's just an option! You don't have to look at me like that."

Juliet tried to think of an appropriate response, but she was still in shock, unable to form a complete sentence. Did her friends really think of her as being on the path to spinsterhood? She supposed Finn was right, but she'd never have put it in those outdated words.

And she'd never, in a million years, pictured herself getting artificially inseminated with her gay friend's sperm so she could bear his child.

This day had officially gotten too weird for her, and it wasn't even three o'clock. She heard the laughing and chatter in the next room, and for the first time she could remember, she wanted to be anywhere but at a party.

AFTER LAST NIGHT, Cole was pretty sure he'd never think of the phrase "secret garden" the same way again. It had gone from reminding him of an innocent children's story to an erotic fantasy in a matter of a few breathy whispers.

He should have spent the day reading the rest of the research proposals his students were expecting back, but instead, he'd wandered around his house full of nervous energy, cleaning things that didn't need cleaning, until he'd finally decided to go for a run. Six miles later, he'd returned home sweaty but no less preoccupied with memories of the night before.

Now his house was more spotless than it had been in years, and the dinner he'd prepared based on Delia's step-by-step instructions for foolproof lasagna was baking in the oven. He usually ate carry-out, but for reasons he didn't care to examine, he'd been determined to make dinner for

Juliet, even going so far as preparing Delia's signature balsamic vinaigrette dressing for the salad.

When his doorbell rang at a few minutes past six, he felt like a nervous schoolboy eager to impress the pretty new girl in his class. Ridiculous, but there it was.

Cole opened the front door and took in the sight of Juliet on his doorstep, dressed for seduction. He had to give her credit—she knew how to look irresistible. With her long hair draped over her bare shoulders, a black dress accentuating her curves, and legs just as smooth and long as in his fantasies, she was a vision of temptation.

He smiled. "You look great."

She gave him a once-over. "Thanks. So do you."

Cole stepped aside and she came in, inhaled the cooking smells, and grinned. "You actually cooked for me?"

He shrugged and told a blatant lie. "It was no big deal. I just threw something together."

What was it about Juliet that brought out the liar in him?

She sauntered into his living room and looked around. Cole tried to imagine the place through her eyes. A decorator he was not, but he thought his place looked better than the typical bachelor pad. What he lacked in decorating flair, he felt like he'd made up for in restoring the hardwood floors, painting the walls a nice gray-blue and getting the place into top shape.

Anyway, why did he care what she thought of his house? He wasn't going to analyze that right now, either.

"This is a nice place," she said, and then her gaze fell on a family photo sitting on the fireplace mantle. It was a group shot of everyone at Christmas, a picture Cole loved for the way it captured all the boisterous charm of his oversize family.

"Wow, are these all your relatives?" she asked as she approached the photo.

"Yeah, those are the close ones—my brothers and their wives and kids."

"Looks like a fun group. One thing I always missed about it just being me and my aunt was big family get-togethers during the holidays."

"You don't have any other relatives?"

She shook her head. "My aunt always had a gathering of friends to celebrate Thanksgiving and Christmas, but it wasn't the same. She had some pretty odd friends, too—odd to a little kid, anyway. I'd probably appreciate them more now."

She sat down on the brown leather sofa and her gaze fell on the stack of papers he'd yet to grade.

"Students' essays?" she asked.

He sighed. "Really they're proposals on what they plan to accomplish in their research projects this semester."

"Sounds exciting," she said with a funny little look that made it clear she thought they were anything but.

"Yeah, it's pretty dry reading, but I've learned that if I don't get them started thinking about their projects now, at the end of the term I'll have a big pile of hastily written garbage to read."

She smiled. "I remember turning in my share of hastily-written garbage in college." And then she gave him a scandalous look. "I'll bet you did, too, Dr. Matheson."

"I'll never admit it. If my students found out, they'd never let me live it down."

"Do you like teaching college?" she asked.

"I like sharing my professional experiences with people who are interested, especially students. They're generally upper-level students, so they're very enthusiastic for the most part."

"And how about your day job?"

"It suits me. I love seeing results, seeing that I've helped an organization through a successful transition."

Cole glanced at his watch and saw that the lasagna had another ten minutes to cook. "Can I get you a drink?" he asked.

"Sure, if you'll let me help."

She followed him into the kitchen and peered into the oven. "You made lasagna? I may have to kiss you for that."

As he was reaching for a glass, he felt her hand slide around his waist. His body temperature rose several degrees. When he turned to face her, she molded her body to him and gave him a wicked little smile.

"I think I may have to start cooking more often," he said, "if this is the thanks I get."

"This is just the start. I've got much more appreciative moves in mind."

He'd had every intention of keeping them out of bed tonight, giving them a chance to get to know each other intellectually instead of physically. But he felt himself grow hard, and then he dipped his head to kiss her.

To hell with restraint, to hell with dinner, to hell with everything. He wanted her here and now.

His conscience made one last nagging plea, but the feel of her body, the lure of her kiss—arguments for restraint didn't stand a chance against them.

He lifted her and set her on the kitchen counter, then pushed her dress up around her waist and admired the delicate white satin panties she wore. They were pretty, but they'd have to go. When he massaged her through the panties with his thumb, she closed her eyes and sighed, spread her legs for him and pushed herself against his hand.

He felt her grow damp through the satin, and a moment later he'd removed her panties and had unhindered access to her. He plunged his fingers inside her and felt that she was hot and ready. She let the straps of her dress fall off her shoulders, and the hint of her cleavage made him want to see more, so he pushed her dress all the way down and had the pleasure of discovering she wasn't wearing a bra. He tasted each bare, delicious breast, taking his time on each one.

Juliet tangled her fingers in his hair, then lifted his face to hers, kissed him with all her hot intensity until he couldn't take it anymore. He wanted her, but he also wanted to savor the experience. They needed to slow down, just a little, just long enough to make it count.

When he broke the kiss, he whispered, ''Let me taste you.''

She smiled a slow, seductive smile, and then he knelt down and buried his tongue inside her.

Dinner all but forgotten, he could think of no hunger besides the one he had for her, and he thrust his tongue in and out, then massaged her clit until she bucked and cried out, until she was so wet and tense he knew she was about to come.

Then he pushed her over the edge, drank her in as she cried out with each spasm of pleasure, savored the feel of her in his hands and in his mouth.

A moment later, he trailed kisses up her belly as he stood up. When he reached her mouth, she clung to him, kissing him as she unfastened his pants and gripped his rigid erection. Without asking, she found his wallet in his back pocket and removed a condom, tore open the package without breaking their kiss, and slid it on him. He liked that trick better every time she did it.

He could wait no longer. He lifted her off the counter and turned her around, then molded their bodies together again as he leaned her over the counter and found her hot, wet opening from behind. Then he plunged inside her. Gripping her hips, he made love to her fast and hard, matching her intensity with his own.

His release came before he could stop it, rocking his body uncontrollably as he clung to Juliet, spilling into her. Slowly he became aware of the smell of lasagna that filled the air, and realized he was supposed to have taken it out of the oven.

He kissed the soft skin on the middle of her back, then pushed her hair aside and kissed her neck, pulling her against him. When he slid his hands up to her breasts and cupped them, she expelled a sigh.

"What an appetizer," she said.

"Wait until you have the main course," he whispered, then nipped at her earlobe.

"Smells like it might be burning."

"That's not the one I was talking about, but you're right," he said, hating himself even as he said it. Sex had become their standard greeting, and now that he was coming down from the high of making love to her, he despised his own lack of self-control.

What had happened to all his resolve? It amazed him that a glimpse of Juliet's flesh and stroke of her hand, could make him toss aside all his good intentions.

Reluctantly, he pried himself away from her and disposed of the condom, then pulled himself together and washed his hands.

Juliet found an oven mitt on the counter and removed the lasagna, which had definitely gotten a little too brown.

"Looks like we're just in time," she said. "I like my cheese crispy anyway."

Cole was having a hard time caring about the cheese or anything else except taking Juliet to bed and spending the rest of the night with her in his arms.

They ate dinner, and Juliet made a big deal over his culinary skills, such as they were. Cole even managed to be a little impressed with himself for having produced a meal that tasted pretty good.

After dinner, she insisted on helping clean up, even though he'd intended to just leave the dishes for tomorrow. Tonight, he was too keyed up from having Juliet in his house to care about a little mess. As she was drying her hands on a dish towel, he took her wrist and pulled her against him.

"Now, I think it's about time we get to know each other better with our clothes on."

She smiled and tossed aside the towel. "But I'm really enjoying helping you further scientific knowledge."

"Our research can never be complete if we don't give ourselves a chance to have a real relationship."

She gave him a pouty look but didn't argue. "I think I can be a patient subject. What sort of research do you have in mind for tonight?"

His body ached for her, but his mind was putting on the brakes. He wanted to get to know her outside of bed, too, but the chemistry between them was so strong, he was nearly helpless to fight it.

He had to think of something that would keep his mind out of the bedroom if he wanted to keep *them* out of the bedroom. But if Juliet suspected that's what he was trying to do, she'd probably walk out the door and never look back.

"I've got this revolutionary idea—we could just sit and talk to each other."

"A little verbal foreplay, then?" She smiled, then placed a lingering kiss on his neck.

Cole's flesh responded to her kiss, but he focused his brain on benign thoughts—taxes, football team stats, anything but Juliet.

"Why don't we go relax in the living room, and you can tell me a little more about your work?" he said.

Talking about party planning couldn't lead them to have sex, could it? It seemed like a safe topic, and he really was curious about her work.

"Why? Because you love parties so much and find the subject endlessly fascinating?"

"I find you endlessly fascinating."

"Well, since you put it that way..." She moved her mouth to his ear and licked his earlobe.

Cole nearly lost all his newfound resolve in a split second. He did want to get to know Juliet better, but his body burned for a very specific kind of acquaintance. He'd never had a harder time staying out of bed with a woman in his life. And if the ache inside him continued to grow at this rate, it was going to be a long, frustrating night.

8

*The League of Scandalous Women's Guiding Principle 8:
A scandalous woman is never scandalous for
the sake of scandal alone. She creates
controversy for a greater purpose.*

JULIET SMILED TO HERSELF as Cole led her from the kitchen into the living room. She'd never dated a guy who'd cooked for her before, and she found it incredibly sexy. Charming, too, like so many other things about Cole.

Like too many things about him.

Her smile disappeared as she realized how easy it would be to fall for him—too easy, if she didn't keep her guard up. Right now, she had a feeling he was trying his best to seduce her outside of bed, to convince her that she was headed down the path of self-destruction or whatever he called it in psychology terms.

That was surely the greatest danger of falling for Cole. He didn't see her as a woman so much as he saw her as a challenge. He'd come to her thinking she could be his pet project, someone he could save from what he'd deemed unhealthy behavior. Once he'd made her see the error of her ways, then what?

His job would be done. So no matter how gorgeous and charming and great in bed he was, she'd be making a mistake if she ever allowed herself to think of him as anything more than a temporary lover.

"I forgot to tell you earlier," he said when they sat down on the sofa. "I talked to the inspector and gave him your number. He'll call you on Monday to set up a time to do the inspection."

"Thanks." Panic settled in Juliet's belly. Getting the house inspected would confirm the work that had to be done and reinforce all the responsibility that came with it.

Scary stuff.

"You look a little pale. I hope it wasn't my cooking."

"I'm having a little panic attack over the thought of keeping the house, that's all."

"If it really scares you, just look at it this way—you can sell the place anytime. Now, during renovations, after renovations. You'll have people lined up to make offers on it, especially after it's been restored."

"You're right. I don't know why I'm so afraid of keeping it."

She slipped off her shoes and started to tuck her feet up under herself on the couch, but Cole pulled her legs onto his lap and started doing something incredible with her shin muscles. She'd never realized how much tension she had stored there until he began the massage.

"Mmm. That feels heavenly."

"For a lot of people, owning a house is a hugely symbolic issue. Maybe you're just afraid of all the things it represents to you."

She closed her eyes and let her head fall back on the couch's headrest as tension drained from her legs. "Are you psychoanalyzing me?"

"Sorry," he said, and she could hear the smile in his voice. "Bad habit."

"It's okay. I'd love to hear what houses are supposed to represent symbolically. Maybe I'll figure out why I'm such a basket case."

"Symbols are highly personal. They're only meaningful insofar as they mean something to you. So, you tell me what a house represents."

"Wow, are you like, a psychologist or something?" She opened her eyes and grinned at him.

He looked delicious in the soft lamplight, with the several days' growth of beard that he'd also worn in one of the photos his brother had brought her of him. The beard softened the hard lines of his jaw and gave him a scruffy, bad-boy look that was entirely at odds with his usual *GQ* image.

"You're using humor to avoid the important issue."

She groaned and stretched out longer on the sofa. "Your questions are too hard."

"Maybe so, but don't you think you'd be happier if you understood the answers?"

Okay, okay. Maybe he was right. Juliet closed her eyes again and tried to think of what exactly the house represented to her. Lots of things came to mind.

She answered without worrying about the consequences. "Commitment, stability, family… Responsibility. Settling down, being tied down—and not in a bondage kind of way. Having fewer options in my life…"

"Whoa, that's a plateful. Let's stop there and talk about all that."

"Why are you doing this?"

"Doing what?"

"Trying to fix me." She opened her eyes again and pinned him with her gaze.

He stared back with a sexy little smile curving his mouth. "It's my job."

"I'm not a paying client."

"No, but you've more than caught my interest. I want to get to know you, how you think, what makes you tick. Sorry if I come off sounding like a psychologist."

She couldn't help but feel flattered. It was rare to meet someone who was really interested in her, and not the way she looked or what she wore or how well she could liven up a party.

She smiled. "You just can't help it, hmm?"

"I'm a lost cause. I analyze everything to death."

"I guess you're waiting for me to get back to the subject. Me and my house issues?"

"You don't have to talk about it if you don't want to. I'm just interested."

Oddly, she did want to talk about it. Cole was about as interested an audience as she was ever going to get. "I get this weird icky feeling in my stomach when I think of all that house-associated stuff."

"Do you think it has anything to do with your not having grown up in a traditional family?"

"Why would it?"

"Sometimes what we know is what we're comfortable with."

Juliet smiled, feeling like she was in one of those cliché movie scenes with the patient reclined on a sofa, pouring out her life story to the therapist. Of course, most therapists weren't as hot as Cole, nor could they give such incredible leg massages.

"But I know that house," she said. "I grew up in it." It had been a part of her life for as long as she could remember, and she realized only now how strange it was that she hadn't wanted to keep it.

"Do you think, though, that at a more basic level, you're afraid to commit to anything so permanent as a house?"

"Sure, maybe."

"Is it possible that fear of committing stems from the impermanence of your original family, your mother and father and you?"

"I don't see how."

"What happens to us in our early childhood can have lifelong and sometimes unpredictable repercussions."

Juliet gave the idea some thought. She had no memories of her father, and very faded ones of her mother. Most of her memories came from photos Ophelia had shown her over the years, along with stories she'd told, few as they were. Ophelia had believed there was no sense in looking back, especially at a history as sad as that of Juliet's family.

"I guess I've always felt that if I can avoid anything complicated, I can be happy."

"And with everything that house symbolizes for you, it's pretty complicated stuff."

"Yeah." He stopped massaging, and she opened her eyes. "You're pretty good at this. Ever think of doing it professionally?"

"Massage therapy? No way." He grinned. "I'd probably end up having to massage a bunch of hairy old guys."

Juliet laughed at the image. "I meant psychotherapy."

"I've never had much interest in working through clients' personal lives." He ran his finger along the bottom of her foot, sending chills from her toes to her spine. "Just a select few people's."

Juliet felt utterly relaxed, and yet the close contact with Cole had started a warming trend inside her that was quickly growing to a heat wave. She withdrew her legs, then climbed onto his lap facing him.

He exhaled. "This doesn't look like a position meant for talking."

"Doctor, I've got a problem only you can cure." He may have wanted to continue his out-of-bed wooing project, but Juliet knew all sorts of tricks for distracting him.

"Should I dare to ask what it is?"

"There's this ache," she said, pulling up her dress, sliding her hand into her panties. "That starts down here, and only gets worse the closer I get to you."

She began to massage herself, and his gaze lingered on her panties. "Does touching yourself help?"

"A little. But not much."

"Hmm. I don't normally diagnose physical ailments," he said as his hands slid under her skirt and around her hips to her ass.

She was hot and slippery, more than ready for him to bury himself inside her again.

"Can't you make an exception? Just this once, for me?" she whispered, growing breathless.

He said nothing, watching as she continued to touch herself with one hand between her legs and the other exploring her breasts. When she'd begun to fear her little trick wasn't working, he finally answered the question.

"I think I can accommodate you."

He lifted her up onto her feet, and they undressed each other in record time. Once they were both naked, and he'd donned a condom, he gave her a gentle shove onto the couch and climbed on top of her.

His erection pressed against her. ''Is this where it hurts?'' he asked, his voice deliciously strained.

''Mmm-hmm. Right there.''

He pushed into her in one clean thrust, filling her, stretching her, driving her wild. She exhaled a sigh of pleasure, and as he made love to her again, she told herself to relax and enjoy the ride.

But something nagged at her.

Guilt.

She'd used her feminine wiles to get Cole where she wanted him, even though he'd been trying his best to put on the brakes and get to know her.

They spent the rest of the night playing, exploring, having fun, but she couldn't shake that guilty feeling. It threatened to spoil her good time, and there was nothing Juliet hated more than a party killer.

She hadn't intended to fall asleep in Cole's bed, in his arms, but she'd just wanted to escape the feeling of guilt. She awoke startled in the middle of the night and glanced around the strange room. The sound of steady breathing beside her, the feel of Cole's arm wrapped around her waist, clued her in to the fact that she was still in Cole's bedroom. Falling asleep there violated the rule she'd promised herself she wouldn't break again.

She muttered a curse to herself, but the feel of his warm, naked body against her was nearly enough temptation to convince her to stay. Her mind startled clear of the fuzziness of sleep, she could imagine all sorts of fun they could have in the morning. Maybe he'd wake her up with a deliciously lazy round of lovemaking. They could have breakfast in bed, maybe a nice, hot shower together. Then maybe a nice, hot up-against-the-shower-wall sex session.

Her insides heated up, and she ached to snuggle closer to him. Perhaps the movement would wake him, and he'd make slow love to her again right now.

No.

She only needed to recall their last morning-after encounter in the hotel room to know it was a bad idea. Too many messy emotions could get stirred up, and someone would get hurt.

She had to leave.

Juliet forced herself to slide out from under his arm, carefully so as not to wake him. She fumbled around in the dark for her clothes with no luck, then remembered that they'd been discarded in the living room.

A few minutes later, she'd gotten dressed and found her purse. She locked Cole's front door from the inside and slipped out silently into the night, then got into her car and started driving home.

But instead of feeling carefree and exhilarated by a night of great sex, the way she was supposed to, she was plagued by a sense that somewhere she'd gone wrong.

She didn't want to be driving away from Cole's house right now. She wanted to be curled up beside him in his bed, and she wanted to wake up in his arms tomorrow. These weren't longings she'd ever experienced in a casual affair before, and yet here they were.

Maybe it was because Cole was different. Deeper, more thoughtful, more complex than the guys she usually dated.

Everything with him was complicated.

It scared her to think that she'd already gotten caught in a web of complicated emotions and obligations with him, that there'd be no easy way out when their month of pseudoresearch was up. And even scarier was the little part of her that didn't want to run away, that wanted to stay and play forever.

Forever. A concept best reserved for children's stories, and definitely not congruent with Juliet's love life. She didn't do forever. She was a here-and-now kind of girl, and she fully intended to keep it that way.

COLE SLID HIS HAND across the bed, searching for Juliet's warm flesh, but all he felt was the cold sheet. He opened his eyes and looked over to see that she was gone, probably already up and having a cup of coffee.

He yawned and stretched, disappointed not to wake up next to her, but looking forward to finding her there in his house looking deliciously tousled from sleep. Her having spent the night would mark a step forward in their relationship, and he felt as though they'd grown closer last night. They were making progress.

He got up and dressed, then wandered out into the living room, a little wary that he'd heard nothing but silence. He went into the kitchen, and Juliet wasn't there. Nor was she anywhere else in the house, he discovered when he looked around.

Damn it.

Maybe she had an early-morning appointment—on a Sunday? Or maybe she'd tried to wake him to say goodbye, but he'd been sleeping too heavily. *Even though he was a light sleeper?*

Or maybe he needed to face the fact that all their progress had been in his head, that Juliet had left in the middle of the night because she didn't want to face him the morning after.

In the living room again, he sat on the couch where they'd made love the night before and picked up the phone from the end table. He dialed her number and listened to one ring, two rings, three rings...

"Hi, it's not me. It's the machine. Leave a message," a tinny version of Juliet's voice instructed.

"Hey. Where are you? Why'd you leave without saying goodbye? Call me." He hung up the phone and sat listening to the silence.

This was not the way he'd imagined last night that he'd be spending Sunday morning—alone and perplexed, frustrated as hell that Juliet fled like a wild animal when he tried to get close. He'd envisioned them spending the day together, having breakfast, talking over the Sunday paper, walking to the park, doing all the lazy Sunday things he loved to do and realized now he wanted a companion to share them with.

Sure, lots of women had been place-fillers, for months or even years. But none of them had felt like The One. None of them had been women he'd wanted to spend the rest of his life getting to know. None until Juliet, and if she couldn't figure out how great they were together, then maybe he was wrong about her.

Maybe she wasn't The One after all.

Pissed off, he undressed again and showered, determined to get out of the house and keep himself from brooding all day.

A half hour later, he was driving to Max and Delia's house without having bothered to call and ask if they'd mind his dropping in. It was a family tradition to stop by unannounced, and he knew they'd be arriving home from Sunday mass right about now, along with bags of beignets they always picked up on the way.

He parked in the driveway behind their behemoth Suburban and rang the doorbell. A few seconds later, Tyler answered, still dressed in his pajamas, and gave him a high-five before letting him in.

"What's the deal with the pj's, man?"

"Mom's on strike, so no one made us go to mass today."

Cole blinked, the information not quite registering. "She's on what?"

"On strike. Only she's not a union worker, says Dad, so she can't be on strike for real. All's it means is that she's holed up in the guest bedroom reading romance novels and shopping on eBay all day."

Cole looked around at the house and saw that it was a wreck. Dirty socks on the floor, shoes cluttering the foyer, magazines and papers all over the furniture, a strange spill in the middle of the living-room carpet...

"Where's your dad?"

"He's mad at Mom for not doing anything, so he went to work this morning."

"So I guess you don't have any beignets," Cole said, feeling like a jerk for being so concerned about breakfast when his brother's family was clearly falling apart.

"No way, dude. I had to eat some old stale Cheerios for breakfast."

"I think I'll go talk to your mom. Is she awake?"

"Yep, but be careful. She's kind of a nutcase lately."

Cole found his way to the guest bedroom through a maze of laundry piles, discarded Barbie dolls and backpacks.

He'd never realized what a bunch of slobs Max's family was. He knocked on the bedroom door.

"What?" It was Delia's voice, sounding none too pleased to have been disturbed.

"It's Cole. Can I come in?"

"As long as you're not going to ask me to cook you a meal or do your laundry, you can."

Cole grinned as he entered the room. He'd always loved Delia's sense of humor and her positive attitude. She brightened up every room she entered, much like Juliet did. To hear that she'd gone on strike—whatever that meant— had to be serious.

"Would you like some company?"

She put down her book, adjusted her bathrobe and pushed herself up more in bed. "Actually, I would. I haven't talked to anyone all day."

"Want to talk about what's going on here?"

"Not especially."

"Have you seen the rest of the house?" Cole asked as he sat down in a chair near the bed.

"I have to go out there to get food and to leave the house. I've seen it."

"So what's this about a strike?"

"A marriage strike. I'm completely unappreciated around here, and I'm not going back on the job until my ingrate family starts doing their share of the work."

Cole nodded. He'd seen how Delia's efforts kept their family running like a well-oiled machine. It was exhausting to watch, so he could imagine how exhausting it must be to do. "Totally understandable."

"Tell that to your brother."

He laughed. "Max may have some slightly outdated notions about women."

"You're telling me. Your mother, God rest her soul, spoiled the hell out of that man."

"He was always her favorite, as I'm sure you know. Her baby, even if he was the oldest. Do you think the strike is working?"

Delia shrugged. "I don't know, but I'm enjoying the vacation. Give me a beach and a margarita and I'll be in heaven."

"Max has to have realized how much you do, judging by that mess out there."

"You would think, but I'm not sure he's even noticed the mess. Now, let anyone make a mess in the Suburban, and he'll have a heart attack."

Sounded like a plan to Cole. "What are you waiting for? Why don't you let the kids have a little fun in there?"

"Not a bad idea. But that still won't get Max to appreciate me any better."

"Your twenty-year anniversary is coming up. You plan on spending it like this?"

"I hope not. I'd thought my strike would have gotten some kind of improvements around here by now, but it's not looking promising."

"I'll have to have a talk with him."

Delia rolled her eyes and shook her head to let him know how much confidence she had in his chances of talking some sense into Max. "Let's talk about something a little more interesting than me. I want to hear what's going on with you and that cute party planner."

Cole figured if he was going to spill his guts to anyone, it might as well be Delia. She'd given him reliable relationship advice on more than one occasion, and in spite of her bad taste in women for him, he trusted her judgment.

Yet when he considered laying out the whole situation with Juliet to be examined, he hesitated. She'd managed to expose to him his own greatest weaknesses, and he wasn't sure he was quite ready to show them to anyone else.

"It's not looking good," he said, not sure how much more detail he was willing to give.

Delia quirked an eyebrow. "What's the problem? She's pretty, she seems smart and fun, and she definitely knows how to liven up a party."

"She's great. But she's got issues."

"I haven't met a person yet who doesn't have issues. As long as she's attracted to you and you're attracted to her, what's the problem?"

"She's not interested in a relationship. Is that enough of an issue for you?"

Her expression turned incredulous. "Come on, now. Have you *ever* met a woman that wasn't interested in you?"

She was giving him too much credit. "Of course I have."

"She's playing hard to get."

"No, she's seriously not looking."

Delia smiled knowingly. "If that were true, she wouldn't be going out on dates with you."

Cole considered pointing out that if Juliet had her way, they'd never leave the bedroom on their dates, that the only reason they'd been together this weekend was because she'd volunteered to test his made-up sex theory, but that seemed like it would be a violation of her privacy.

He kept his mouth shut. No point in arguing with Delia over this.

"Well, if you want my advice—and who wouldn't?—just keep being your charming self, and she'll eventually fall for you like all the rest have."

Cole decided to ignore her overestimation of his charms with women. He needed her dose of confidence right about now, and if he could just convince Juliet that he was such a great guy, life would be easy.

"What should I think when she sneaks out of my house in the middle of the night without bothering to say good-bye?"

"Not even a note?"

Cole shook his head.

"Maybe she had an early-morning appointment she forgot to tell you about."

"On a Sunday?"

Delia shrugged. "Let her explain before you jump to any conclusions."

Sound advice. But Cole had a feeling he needed to slow down things with Juliet until she was ready to commit to something more than casual sex.

He also needed to direct the conversation well away from his personal life before he did something stupid like blurt out that he was afraid—after having barely gotten to know her outside of bed—he was falling for Juliet.

"So," he said, "Max is at the restaurant?"

"Yep. So far his strategy for dealing with my strike has been to work longer hours."

"I think I'll take a trip over to Blue Bayou and give that brother of mine a talking to."

"Be sure and tell him how incredibly lucky he is to have such a fabulous wife."

"And that he needs to learn how to pick up his own socks?"

She smiled. "Oh yeah, that, too."

Cole left his brother's house and headed for the restaurant. As he drove, he thought about Max and Delia's marriage and how, subconsciously, he'd always held it up as an example of what he hoped to have someday. Even with Delia on strike and Max hiding out at work, he still thought they had a good thing going. He could think of much worse problems to have than theirs.

Like his own, for instance.

9

The League of Scandalous Women's Guiding Principle 9:
A scandalous woman surrounds herself with other
women of like mind, to share ideas and find
renewed strength in their camaraderie.

JULIET TOOK A SIP of espresso and closed her eyes to wait for the hot, smooth liquid dose of caffeine to take effect. After waking up in Cole's bed Saturday night, she'd been edgy, restless and wide awake for the rest of the weekend.

She'd spent Sunday trying to take care of administrative chores for Any Occasion, but half the time she'd found herself staring off into space, thinking about Cole. It had been a long time since a guy had managed to distract her so much she found herself obsessed with thoughts of him.

Definitely not a good sign.

This morning was her coffee date with Delia, and although she would have loved to stay home and catch up on the rest she'd lost, she was looking forward to getting to know Cole's sister-in-law, whom he'd spoken so well of.

Besides, she had work to do today, and she'd gotten a call first thing in the morning from the inspector Cole had recommended. She'd made an appointment to meet with him later today, and she was nervous to find out what he had to say, now that she'd made the decision to keep the house. Part of her wanted to hear that it was termite-infested and needed to be burned to the ground, while another part of her dreaded the idea of hearing that the house had any serious problems.

Around her, the conversation and clattering dish sounds of her favorite café mingled with the sounds of traffic on the road outside the door that was propped open, and she felt oddly soothed by all the noise in contrast to the silence of her apartment. Living alone occasionally had its drawbacks, especially when she was awake and longing for certain male companionship.

All night she'd been plagued by doubts—doubts about her decision to keep her aunt's house, doubts about her ability to resist Cole's outside-the-bedroom charms long enough to prove him wrong, doubts about her choices in life. Was she wrong to want to cling to the single life? Was she setting herself up to be disappointed and bitter in her old age?

These were not the kind of thoughts Juliet cared to linger over. Her happy, carefree fling was turning into anything but, and if she wanted to preserve her sanity and her life as she knew it, she had a feeling she needed to end her relationship with Cole.

The moment the thought formed in her head, she bristled at it. Saturday night had been incredible, as had the other evenings she'd spent with him. She'd had great sex before, but sex with Cole wasn't just great. It was mind-blowing. It was soul-stirring.

That was part of the problem. She hadn't been looking

to get her soul stirred. And now that it had been, she wanted her old unstirred soul back.

No, she had to stand by her word. She'd told Cole she'd give him a month, and she wanted to have this month with him, too. She just needed to believe in herself, stand by her scandalous woman principles, and trust that in the end she'd prove Cole's theory wrong.

Cole had been working double-time Saturday night trying to prove *her* wrong. His efforts to keep them out of bed long enough to do the getting-to-know-each-other thing had been utterly charming.

She'd begun to see how easy it would be to fall for him, which had made her realize she needed to create a fourth rule for painless no-strings-attached flings—make sure your partner is easy to let go of. He can be gorgeous, he can be good in bed, but he can't be the kind of guy you'd want to keep around for long.

Ideally, he should have some kind of obnoxious flaw. Maybe he ate with his mouth open or snored like a chainsaw. It's even more ideal if he had an unfixable flaw like a bland personality or the IQ of a tree monkey.

Unfortunately, Cole was flawless as far as she could tell. Okay, so he hated parties. That could be a flaw, but she was afraid Finn had been right in his assertion that opposites make great partners. She *did* find Cole's calmer, more serious personality fascinating, even soothing. When she was with him, she felt an odd sense of balance that she'd never felt before.

Uneasiness welled up inside her. She didn't want someone to balance her out or settle her down. She wanted the fun, wild life she knew, and Cole posed a serious threat. She had no idea what to do with him.

There was the fact that he was a psychologist, that he was trying to prove she was a basket case. Now *that* was a flaw. Yes, definitely a big one. The last thing she wanted was a boyfriend who saw her as a research subject rather than a woman.

Juliet smiled when she spotted her coffee date walking in. Delia moved with the sort of confidence that suggested she was used to being in charge. Tall and attractive, Juliet estimated she was somewhere around forty years old. She had shoulder-length blond hair and topaz-blue eyes, not to mention curves that managed to be traffic-stopping even after three kids.

Delia spotted Juliet and waved, then headed for the counter to place her order. Once she had coffee in hand, she came and sat down across from Juliet.

"Hi."

"Sorry I'm so late. I just got my hair highlighted for the first time ever, and I had no idea how long it takes."

"No big deal—I'm not in a hurry. Your hair looks great, by the way."

Delia swished her hair around. "Thanks. I couldn't stop admiring it in the rearview mirror on the way here."

"So what made you treat yourself to highlights and a coffee break?"

Delia sighed. "Funny you should ask. I'm on strike against my family."

"On strike as in picketing and refusing to work?"

"Sort of. I'm refusing to do mom and wife duties until they start appreciating my efforts a little more."

Juliet smiled. "Good for you."

She shrugged. "It hasn't been a week yet, but so far, no improvements."

"What if it doesn't work?"

"I didn't think that far ahead. I can't exactly go get a paying day job because I homeschool our youngest, and I'm not ready to put her in regular schools again."

"A night job then?"

Delia made a face. "I just want the strike to work."

"How will you know when it has?"

"When they all coming groveling to me and show me that they've learned to pick up after themselves."

This was exactly the sort of reason Juliet didn't see any reason to rush into marriage. She had no interest in ending up an underappreciated servant.

Delia seemed to read her mind. "Don't get me wrong, I love my family and I generally love my life, but our household just needs a little shake-up."

Juliet smiled. "My aunt always told me that being a parent was like volunteering to swim upstream in a river for the rest of your life—an exhausting task that will get you nowhere."

Delia's eyes widened. "It sounds like she had issues."

Maybe she did. Juliet had never thought to question her aunt's take on parenthood before, but something must have happened that caused her to feel that way.

"I guess having me thrust into her life so unexpectedly might have left her a little bitter."

"Was she good to you?"

"Always. She wasn't a motherly type, but she took good care of me in the best way she knew how."

"Still, she shouldn't have made that parenting comment to you."

"I never really looked at it that way, but now that you mention it, I wonder if she was bitter from having raised my own mother. She was fifteen years older than my mom, so when she was a teenager, my grandmother left a lot of the mothering tasks to her."

"Nothing like having your teen years ruined by a baby to give you an aversion to motherhood."

That made perfect sense, and Juliet had no idea why she'd never connected those parts of her aunt before. "Ophelia was a complex woman, for sure," she said, tucking the information away in her mind to think more about later.

"What about your parents?"

Juliet dismissed the question with a wave of her hand. "Long, depressing story I'll save for another time."

Delia gave her a concerned look but didn't press. "I'm glad we were able to get together like this. I rarely have time to do something just for me, and after my failed girls' night out the other night, I need my social fix."

Juliet smiled. "Cole said you and Max have been married for twenty years?"

"That's right. Our twenty-year anniversary is coming up next month."

"Wow, sounds like fun. What are you doing to celebrate?"

Delia shrugged. "Who knows if we'll even be speaking to each other by then. If we are, we'll probably just be leaving the kids at my mom's house and going out to dinner. That's what we do every year."

"You have to do something special! Let me plan an anniversary party for you with all your friends and family," she offered, immediately realizing she shouldn't have. For one thing, how would she pay for it, and for another, where would she find the time?

"No, I can't let you do that—"

"Yes, you can. Go ahead and have your nice dinner out together, and the next night, you can celebrate with everyone. It'll be fun."

She looked like she was about to be won over, and Juliet couldn't resist pushing her the rest of the way. She'd never been able to let an opportunity to celebrate slip by.

"I don't want you going to any trouble for us."

"But I want to do this. Come on, it'll be fun!"

Delia cast a doubtful look at her. "If you'll let us pay you, maybe I can agree to it."

"Absolutely not! It was my idea."

"Then it's not happening."

Juliet had already decided on her course of action though. If she had to, she'd make it a surprise party.

Delia sipped her coffee, then said, "Why do I get the feeling you're planning to do it anyway?"

Okay, so she was busted. "I don't know what you're talking about."

"If you really insist on throwing a party, please get Cole involved. He'll make sure your costs are covered."

"Okay, fine, if you insist, I'll make sure I ask him to help," Juliet said just to end the standoff. She'd get Cole involved, but it would be to help make the party personal.

"So tell me, what's going on between you and Cole? Anything serious?"

"Definitely not serious."

"Come on, you have to tell me more than that. Trying to get information from Cole is like trying to milk a bull."

Juliet laughed at the image. "Okay, okay. I'm really not in the market for a serious relationship, but Cole isn't taking no for an answer."

"The fact that you've actually got Cole pursuing you is one for the record books."

"Why?"

"He's always been the cool one. I think he's spent his whole life with women chasing him. He's never had to lift a finger to have a girlfriend."

"I can see how that might happen with a hottie like Cole. A little challenge is good for him, then."

Delia smiled sheepishly. "All my matchmaking efforts have been disastrous with him, so I'm thrilled to see him really interested in you. I think you're good for him. I haven't seen Cole so prone to smiling and joking in his life."

Juliet didn't want to burst her bubble by pointing out that she and Cole didn't have a chance of becoming more than lovers. "What do you mean? He's normally a stiff?"

"No, he's just a bit on the serious side. He's got that dark and brooding thing going on, and it's part of his charm, but he could use a little lightening up."

Yet another reason why they were just too different to have more than sex—Juliet didn't do dark and brooding. She liked her guys to be the life of the party. She thought of the way Max and his brothers had told her Cole was a real party animal, and she smiled.

"Your husband told me a few tall tales about Cole to make sure I really spiced up the party for him."

Delia rolled her eyes. "That man…"

"He seems like a great guy. From what Cole has told me about you both, I really admire what the two of you have. I'm kind of surprised about the marriage strike."

Whoa, where had that admiration comment come from? Juliet hadn't realized she was going to say it until the words popped out of her mouth, but now that they were out there, she realized they were true. A lasting marriage was such a rare thing, those who accomplished it deserved praise.

Delia produced a wry smile. "Twenty years of wedded bliss. Seriously though, it's easy to forget how lucky we've been. Thanks for reminding me."

"There aren't many people who can last so long together and still be happy." Juliet thought of her parents' marriage, of many of her friends' parents who were also divorced. Delia and Max were actually one of the few examples she knew of a long-lasting marriage.

She was rooting for Delia's marriage strike to work fast, and she felt even more determined to throw a party to honor what they'd built. And, she realized, if she could be sure her own hypothetical marriage would last and be a happy one, she'd be more open to the idea of it.

Juliet was so shocked by the thought that she quickly shoved it aside to be examined later.

Much later.

"I was looking for anything but a husband back when Max and I met, and Max—he seemed so wrong for me."

"You're kidding, right?"

"Not at all. Thank goodness we both grew up, or we never would have survived as a couple."

"If you weren't looking for marriage, and he was all wrong for you, how did you end up getting married?"

Delia downed the last of her coffee, then answered with a dreamy smile, "I was young and full of romantic notions. Love conquers all, that sort of thing."

Juliet couldn't help but smile, too. "And he swept you off your feet."

"Only so he could get me in a horizontal position, if you know what I mean."

Juliet's smile turned to a laugh. "Isn't that every guy's strategy?"

Every guy except Cole.

She sobered when she realized just how far he'd gone in defying her expectations. Cole turned all her ideas about relationships and sex and men upside down, and she had no idea what to make of him. He was too complicated, too analytical, too sure of his own silly sex theory.

"Anyway," Delia said, "I hope you change your mind about Cole. I think you'd make a great couple."

Juliet just shrugged, not wanting to disappoint her new friend but also not wanting to mislead her.

Delia eyed her. "Come on, tell me—what's *really* going on with you two?"

"It's a sex thing, that's all."

"I don't believe it."

"That's as much as I'm going to say. If you want more, you'll have to go back to milking the bull."

Delia laughed. "No, thanks. I've got enough to keep me busy."

"I can imagine. Three kids, a husband, the restaurant, a marriage strike—"

They both laughed then.

"The restaurant is Max's baby. He takes care of it, and I take care of the kids."

"I'd like to meet your kids sometime."

"Oh, believe me, you will. Why don't you come over to Kelly and Jake's house with Cole for a picnic on Sunday and get yourself a nice big dose of hands-on birth control."

"I'd love to," she said, considering to late that she'd have to face Cole. "Will it be okay with Kelly and Jake?"

"Of course. I'll let them know you're coming."

Delia's comment hit home a little late. *"Birth control?"* Juliet asked.

"I'm not joking. Once you've been around my teenagers, you may never have sex again," she said, though it was apparent by her smile that she didn't believe her own propaganda.

Juliet laughed. "You're not exactly winning me over to the marriage and children camp."

"Well, at the risk of getting mushy, I love being a mom—it's the absolute best thing I've ever done. The good news is, they start out as babies, which are sweet and cuddly and provide absolutely no preparation for what they'll be like when they turn sixteen."

Juliet smiled, and out of nowhere, an idea came to her, something she'd thought of before but cast aside as silly and impractical. "Talking to you, hearing how busy you are, reminds me of what a need there is for women to have girl time."

"Absolutely! I'm so glad we could get together like this. I hope we can do it again soon."

Juliet bit her lip, considering whether she really wanted to do what had been forming in the back of her mind ever since she'd found the list of the League of Scandalous Women's Guiding Principles.

"I've been thinking…. When my aunt was younger, she formed something called The League of Scandalous Women."

"Ooh, I love it already," Delia said.

"It was a group of women who met once a month at my aunt's house, to talk, socialize, celebrate being the wild women of their time. Wouldn't it be great to have something like that again?"

"Regularly scheduled girl time? Sounds too good to be true."

"I've got a lot of friends who are in your situation now that they're married and have kids. I never get to see them anymore."

Delia nodded. "I've lost touch with a lot of my girlfriends over the years. It's hard to keep up when our lives take different directions."

"But if you had a regular time to get together each month, I bet you wouldn't have lost touch."

"Are you really thinking of starting up this scandalous women's group again?" Delia leaned forward in her seat, propping her elbows on the table and smiling like she couldn't wait to hear more.

"I am. I just think it's too good an idea to let it fade into history."

"And Cole mentioned that you're keeping your aunt's

house and renovating it. Would you have the meetings there every month?"

"It *is* the tradition."

"Wow, sounds like a lot of fun. Count me in, and let me know if you can use any help."

"I already know a way you can help. I want the group to start out small, but I'd like to have women of a variety of ages and backgrounds. If you know anyone who fits the bill as a scandalous woman and you think they'd like to come, let me know, and we can invite them."

"Ooh, I do have a few scandalous friends I'd love to get together with again."

Juliet glanced at her watch and realized she had exactly fifteen minutes to make her appointment with the inspector at Ophelia's house. "I've gotta run, but I'm really glad we got together," she said as she stood up.

"And you'll come to the picnic Sunday?"

"Definitely," she said, though she felt a stab of something—apprehension?—in her belly.

She had a feeling that in spite of Delia's marriage strike, she was living a good life, with a great family. Would seeing such a perfect example of familial bliss make Juliet long to have the same thing?

And what if it did? Why did the idea bother her so much?

Because she knew it was too rare to hope for, too unrealistic a dream. She'd stick with the happy, uncomplicated life she knew and leave family entanglements for braver women than she.

DELIA STARED out the window of the coffee shop, watching as Juliet disappeared down the sidewalk. She recognized so much of herself in Juliet, it was uncanny. But for a few different life choices, she could have been in an identical spot as Juliet ten years ago. She could have been the one living the single life, running from commitment, uncertain of the future.

Had she missed out by choosing to marry so young? Before her kids, she'd occasionally had her moments of doubt, but now, she realized, she didn't envy Juliet.

Even in her current marriage strike predicament, she couldn't imagine changing the decisions she'd made that had led her to this place in life. A sudden, unexpected wave of emotion welled up inside her, and she had to blink away the dampness in her eyes. She'd never expected talking to Juliet would make her appreciate the life she had.

But it had. And now if she could just get her family to appreciate *her* a little more, she'd be okay.

Delia wasn't ready to leave the comfortable clatter of the coffee shop, so she went back to the counter and ordered a second cup, then returned to the table trying not to feel guilty that she wasn't doing something more productive than sitting around drinking coffee.

As she watched the traffic on the street outside, her thoughts returned to Juliet and Cole. Her gut told her those two belonged together. They balanced each other out, and if they could just learn to appreciate each other's differences, she could really see them being happy together. It was a shame Juliet didn't get that.

Balance. Once upon a time, she and Max had achieved it perfectly. He was the stable one, the hard worker, the devoted lover. And Delia had been the wild one, the fun-loving one, the one who'd kept the spark alive in their relationship.

So how had she turned into a frustrated, unappreciated homemaker? She'd let it happen. She'd grown complacent, she'd gotten too busy, too wrapped up in her kids. She was as much to blame as anyone for her problems.

From inside her purse, her cell phone rang. Delia dug around until she found it and saw on the LCD that it was her daughter Brianna, calling on her own new cell phone, which she'd begged and pleaded for almost daily for the past year until they gave in and got her one for her birthday over the summer.

"Hi, Brie."

"Hi, Mom. It's lunchtime here, and I was just thinking...."

Here it came. A request to stay out late—forbidden on a school night—or go to a friend's house after school. Those were the only reasons she ever called.

"Thinking what?" she said when her daughter didn't continue.

"About you."

"What about me?"

"I guess, you know, with you going on the marriage strike thing, I've been feeling kind of bad about how you do so much work for us, and we, like, don't really appreciate it."

Huh? Delia blinked. Had she just heard her daughter correctly? Had someone in her family finally gotten the point?

"Well, I guess that's the point I've been trying to make."

"I just wanted to say I'm sorry. I promise I'll clean my room tonight."

"Thanks, Brie. I'd really like that."

"Guess I'd better go. Lunch is almost over."

It was probably hoping for too much to think her teenage daughter would want to spend an evening with her, but she had to ask, "Want to go out for dinner and ice cream with me tonight?"

"Um, sure. Can I order my own fudge brownie sundae?"

"Absolutely."

When Delia ended the call and put the phone back in her purse, she was fully aware that she was wearing a goofy grin. If nothing else good came of her marriage strike, it would have been worth it, just to hear Brianna say she appreciated her mother's efforts.

Finally, some small bit of vindication. One family member down, and three more to go.

"JULIET? THIS IS COLE again. Are you going to return any of my calls? Delia said you're supposed to be going to the family picnic on Sunday, so call me if you are."

Cole hung up the phone and winced at the angry-desperate tone he was afraid his voice had taken on. Great, now she'd think he was stalking her.

He put the phone down on his desk and sighed, staring at his computer screen. He was too edgy to work tonight, too keyed up from thinking about Juliet.

All week, he'd considered stopping by her office or her aunt's house, forcing her to face him. He figured at the very least he deserved an explanation of her behavior since last Saturday, but in the end, he'd practiced avoidance by working late and putting in extra hours advising students on their projects. It had kept him distracted, until now.

He'd even managed to feel guilty that he'd promised to help her with the house, and nearly a week had passed without his lifting a finger. He knew she needed to get the house ready to move into as soon as possible. It was her fault for not returning his call, but still.

He stood up from his desk and stalked around the room, looking for a book or a magazine—anything to take his mind off of her, but instead, he found himself wandering around the house. Nearly every room brought to his mind an erotic image of what he'd done with Juliet here last weekend, and now it was Friday night and he was home alone under the guise of working.

He'd turned down an invitation from some friends to go to a sports bar, turned down an invitation from his brother Paul to come over for dinner and turned down an invitation from a woman he barely knew in passing to go out with her. And now he was sitting home alone and hating himself for it.

He stalked into his bedroom and undressed, put on his jogging gear, and then headed out the door, hoping he could pound thoughts of Juliet out of his head with a good, hard run.

Five miles later, he was drenched in sweat, and his heart was pounding, but there was still only one woman on his mind. One sexy-as-sin, frustrating-as-hell woman.

Cole went to the extra bedroom he'd set up as a workout room and lifted weights for what must have been an hour, then took a shower, pulled on a pair of shorts, and collapsed on the couch with a stack of students' papers to grade.

He started reading the paper on top, and after a minute or two, he realized he hadn't comprehended a word he'd read. Instead, his thoughts had wandered to Juliet's disappearance from his bed last weekend.

What raw spot had he touched inside her to make her run scared? Was she really so afraid of their getting to know each other? Was she really so unwilling to give them a chance?

No point in speculating. But he couldn't help it. If she was really that easily spooked, then maybe he'd been way off in his belief that they had something worth exploring. Maybe he was a fool to let himself fall for her.

Okay, he was definitely a fool. He couldn't deny it.

The scary thing was, knowing he was headed in the wrong direction pursuing Juliet didn't make him turn around and go a different way. He was still in the driver's seat, still totally aware that he was on a collision course, and if it meant having her for himself, he wasn't sure he cared about the self-destruction.

10

*The League of Scandalous Women's Guiding Principle 10:
A scandalous woman admits her mistakes, learns
from them, even celebrates them. She knows that
without failure, there can be no success.*

JULIET LISTENED to Cole's message a second time, then deleted it. The right thing to do was to call him back. She should definitely call him back. But every time she thought of picking up the phone, she recalled her sense of panic Saturday night, and she couldn't do it.

She was still standing next to the phone when it rang and nearly scared her to death. She took a deep breath to calm her pounding heart and started to pick up the phone, then hesitated. What if it was Cole? What would she say to him?

It didn't matter. She'd have to talk to him sooner or later, so now was as good a time as any.

"Hello?"

"Hey, Juliet, it's Delia."

Oh, thank God. "Hi, Delia. I thought you were someone else."

"Someone as in my brother-in-law?"

"No," Juliet lied, then felt guilty. "Yes."

"He said he didn't know if you were coming to the picnic with him Sunday, so I figured I'd ask you myself."

"Oh, right, the picnic. I've been so busy this week I nearly forgot."

And maybe she hadn't exactly wanted to think about attending a family get-together with Cole.

"Are you two on the outs?"

"Is that what he told you?"

"Cole was his usual tight-lipped self. I'm hoping you'll enlighten me."

Juliet's mouth went dry for reasons she couldn't have explained. "I've just been too busy to get in touch with him, that's all."

"I thought he was going to help you with renovating the house?"

"I hate asking that big a favor of anyone."

"Juliet, when an able male wants to help you, and he's as great a guy as Cole is, you don't say no."

She did need the help. She'd picked out paint and bought it, applied for her loan, had someone come give her an estimate on replacing the windows, and browsed through a few home improvement stores looking at updated kitchen and bathroom fixtures. But when it came to actually getting started on the real work, she didn't have a clue where to begin.

Finn hadn't been much help. His interest in home improvement only extended as far as watching it on the Home and Garden channel.

"Okay, okay. I'll call him tonight."

"I just talked to him a few hours ago, and it sounded like he was sitting home alone. Is that what you're doing, too?"

It sounded so pitiful when she put it like that. "Well, I was supposed to be going out with a friend, but her fiancé caught a flight here from San Diego at the last minute, so yeah, I guess I am."

"Do I actually have to point out to you that it might be a good idea to pay Cole a visit?"

"I was just thinking I'd stay in and watch a movie."

"You can watch a movie just as easily at his house as you can at yours."

"Are you playing matchmaker or what?"

"Of course I am. I don't know what you two had a falling-out over, but it can't be anything that bad. You're both good people, and I'll bet you're great together. You just need to get a clue and figure that out for yourselves."

Juliet smiled. She loved Delia's straightforwardness, even if she didn't always agree with what she said. And in this case, she really did owe Cole a visit. It took someone else pointing it out to motivate her.

"Okay, okay. I'll drop by his house if you'll quit nagging me."

"Good, and wear something sexy."

She'd wear something that would make him forget all about the fact that'd she'd been avoiding him all week.

"So," Juliet said, "how goes the marriage strike?"

Delia sighed into the phone. "I'm beginning to think I'll have to move out to get any kind of progress at this rate."

"Wow, it's that bad?"

"The kids keep knocking on the door asking me for things— 'Mom, where's my red shirt? Mom, I need a ride to soccer practice. Mom, I need, I need, I need.' And Max picked the lock on the guest bedroom door last night and came in to have a talk with me."

"A good talk or a bad talk?"

"He told me he was going to hire a maid service until I was ready to go back on the job."

"Uh-oh, calling in hired help isn't good."

"I told him the whole point of my strike was to get *him and the kids* to do some work around the house. I'm going to strangle that man."

"Maybe he'd let you keep the maid service for good?"

"Um, I think not. I got a little verbally abusive, and perhaps hit below the belt with some comments about his bedroom techniques."

"Uh-oh." Juliet couldn't help but smile.

"Yeah, I may have gone too far this time. But I think I finally got his attention."

"Let me know if there's any way I can help, okay?"

Delia laughed. "I may need a couch to sleep on soon."

"I hope it doesn't come to that, but you're welcome to mine. What can I bring to the picnic? And will you even be there?"

"Oh sure, I love Max's family—I'm not on strike against them. Why don't you just bring some potato salad?"

"Will do. Guess I'd better head over to Cole's house before it gets too late."

Delia sighed. "Have fun. At least I can rest assured *someone* is tonight."

After she hung up the phone, Juliet hurried around her bedroom trying to get herself put-together. She'd been running errands all day, helping Rebecca pick out wedding invitations and meeting with a furniture restorer to look at some of Ophelia's antiques that were in bad condition. Now she hardly felt fit to show up on Cole's doorstep.

With a little makeup, a hair brushing and a change of

clothes—out of her work attire and into her traffic-stopper pants and matching top—she looked almost refreshed, and she was out the door and on her way.

As she drove, she sang along to the music on the radio— anything to avoid thinking about the rising panic that came with the idea of being in Cole's house again. She wasn't exactly proud of the way she'd snuck out and then spent the week avoiding him, but she'd gotten a glimpse of how comfortable, how right, Cole could be, and it had thrown her off kilter.

Comfortable equaled trapped, tied down, and eventually boring as hell. She'd end up like Delia, locked in a guest bedroom on strike against a family who didn't appreciate her if she wasn't careful.

Cole lived in a historic neighborhood not far from hers, and his own house had clearly been restored with care. Even in the dark, she could tell he'd put a lot of effort into the exterior and landscaping.

She stood on the doorstep, her heart pounding and her stomach revolting against the idea of ringing the doorbell. But the warm light pouring through the front window seemed to welcome her, and she relaxed a bit.

When she finally rang the bell, she wondered what she'd been so afraid of. Cole was just a man, and as the scandalous woman she was supposed to be, she should have been facing whatever fears he brought out in her, not cowering from them.

Really, she shouldn't have been afraid at all, because last weekend hadn't meant a thing. *She* had control over her emotions, not Cole.

It was like Ophelia always said, a woman had to figure out what she wanted and then put all of herself into going after it. If Juliet wanted a hot, temporary fling with Cole, that's what she'd have, one way or another.

She heard footsteps in the foyer, and then he opened the door and stood there looking like her fantasy come to life. He wasn't wearing a shirt, just a pair of loose-fitting gym shorts, and his hair was still damp from a shower.

To think that only a few thin pieces of fabric stood between them…

Juliet gave herself a mental slap. Cole was just too damn sexy, and he dragged her thoughts straight to the bedroom.

He pinned her with his intense blue gaze and didn't say a word. Clearly, he hadn't appreciated her disappearing act.

"I'm sorry," she offered lamely. "It's been a crazy week."

"A phone call only takes a minute."

"Are you going to give me a guilt trip or invite me in so I can grovel properly?"

A smile played on his lips. "If you're going to grovel, I guess you can come in."

Oh, she had all sorts of ways in mind to show him her remorse. Hot, sexy ways…

There she went again, thinking sex.

He escorted her into the living room, where the weekend before, they'd done exactly what she'd just been thinking about. He perched himself on the arm of the couch and crossed his arms over his bare chest, causing his pectoral muscles to flex in a way that made Juliet salivate. Her gaze traveled lower, to the ridges of his ab muscles, and she had to sit down.

"I'm waiting," he said.

Juliet gave him a blank look.

"For you to start groveling."

"Oh." She smiled. "Right. Well, have I apologized yet? I have, haven't I? Hmm…"

The truth was, she was awful at groveling. In fact, she pretty much made it a rule not to do it, no matter how far in the wrong she'd been. But she did have ways of expressing that she was sorry….

He scratched his temple. "Is this the best you can do?"

"You're right, I can do better." She stood up from her seat and went to him. "I just can't do it sitting across the room from you."

She positioned herself between his legs, traced her fingertips along the waistline of his shorts and looked him in the eye with her best do-me look.

He stiffened, and not in a good way. "I hope you didn't just come here to have sex."

Tough audience. "No, I didn't. I came here to apologize. I just prefer to express myself physically, okay? Do you want to inhibit my self-expression?"

There. He was a psychologist. Maybe he'd buy that story.

"Why did you disappear last Saturday night?"

"I didn't disappear. I just went home."

His gaze turned a few degrees cooler. "You know what I mean."

"Let's remember the ground rules. Don't you recall that one of them states very clearly, 'no spending the night'?"

"I think we need to get rid of those rules."

"They're in place to protect us from situations like this—if we both keep them in mind."

Cole stared at her but said nothing.

"I volunteered myself to help further scientific knowledge. We're supposed to be having casual sex, so long as I'm open to the idea of something more.''

"How can there be the possibility of anything more if all we do is have sex?''

"We've done things together besides have sex.''

A few things.

"Like what?''

Juliet needed a distraction, and quick. "Why don't you tell me more about your Theory of Sexual Relativity. I'd be interested to hear if you've revised it at all since you met me.''

"I'd say you're proving it right, so far.''

"How so?'' Juliet asked, fully expecting him to launch into a list of the reasons she was an emotionally damaged person. As far as his theory went though, she didn't buy it. She'd bet it was just a bunch of psychological mumbo-jumbo, created purely for Cole's convenience.

"You're doing everything you can to keep an emotional distance from me, in spite of the fact that we'd both benefit from getting closer.''

"I don't see how that's necessarily true. What if we did get closer? Then what? We break up later and one or both of us gets hurt.''

He seemed to be considering his words before he spoke. "We'd both be richer for having known each other.''

"Doesn't your theory deal with breakups?''

He shrugged. "I'm still in the process of refining it.''

"Right. So basically, no matter what happens, you'll find a way to prove your theory correct.''

"I didn't say that.''

"But if you're still refining it, as you say—''

"Stop trying to dodge the real issue here.'' His expression said he still wasn't ready to forgive her for leaving last weekend. "I don't see what any of this has to do with you leaving here without saying goodbye."

"I didn't want to wake you up."

"You could have stayed the night."

"And that is exactly what I didn't want to do. There's no chance of keeping this casual if I keep spending the night with you."

"*Keep* spending the night?"

"It would have been two weekends in a row, and the first time was disastrous enough for us to figure out that it shouldn't happen again."

Cole didn't look convinced, but he didn't protest, either. He simply looked down at her fingers still tracing the waistline of his shorts and then back up at her.

"We're not having sex," he said, and in spite of the heat she felt at her fingertips, a cold wave hit her.

But Juliet prided herself on not being a quitter. "We don't have to. I'm supposed to be here showing you how sorry I am, anyway."

"Yeah, I'm still waiting to see that," he said.

Juliet had every intention of giving him an eyeful.

She looked around the room. "You know, we were so busy last Saturday night, I never got a chance to see your whole house. Want to show me around?"

His gaze turned suspicious, but he nodded. Juliet let her hand drop away from him, and she stepped back and followed as he led her out of the room.

She peeked into his bathrooms and closets, surveyed each room to see what it revealed about Cole's personality. Everything was neat and in its place, the decor masculine but not hard-edged. His office surprised her the most.

''I chose this house because of the in-law suite,'' he said as he flipped on the light.

Juliet noticed the door leading outside, providing a separate entrance to the room from the driveway. ''So your clients can come here without seeing your personal space.''

''Exactly.''

''I've been trying to picture what your office looks like. I was way off.''

''How so?''

''I didn't realize you worked from home, for one. And I pictured something more high-tech, with lots of chrome and black leather.''

''That kind of decor doesn't exactly encourage clients to relax.''

''How often do your clients come here?''

''Not often. I usually go on-site to whatever business has hired me, but occasionally for the initial contact, clients come here.''

''Must be great to work at home.''

''It's nice, but it has its drawbacks. For one, I always feel like I should be working whenever I have any spare time.''

''You're a workaholic, perhaps?''

''I may have slight tendencies toward it,'' he said.

Juliet strolled around the office, reading book spines and looking at the various stuff he had on display. He'd filled his office shelves with art objects, books and memorabilia, probably a psychologist's tactic to make the place feel more welcoming and personal, and it had worked. She could imagine sitting here and pouring out her innermost thoughts to Cole.

"You like baseball?" she asked, looking at his autographed ball collection.

"'Like' might be too mild a term."

"Ah, so you're part of the cult of baseball."

"Card-carrying member," he said, grinning.

"I'm sort of a fan myself. Bet you wouldn't have guessed that." She turned and regarded him curiously.

"I've learned not to make too many assumptions about people. I'm rarely right anyway."

"Come on—a psychologist not making assumptions? I don't believe it." She sat down on the couch and settled in, propping her feet up on the coffee table and stretching her arms along the back of the couch.

"Okay, I *try* not to. Is that better?"

She smiled. Now it was time to show him how sorry she was and hopefully get rid of that chilly look in his eyes.

"Now tell me," she said, sliding her hand across the buttery surface of the leather sofa. "What do I have to do to get you to act out a hot professor-coed fantasy with me?"

Cole's wary expression remained. "A what?"

"You can be the professor, and I'll be the naughty coed."

"I told you, we're not having sex tonight."

He was leaning against the desk, and she stood up and went to him, got as close as she could get without touching. "Who said anything about sex? There are all sorts of ways to act out a fantasy."

He finally gave in and let a half smile soften his glare. "I can only think of one way that would be any fun."

"Then you lack imagination. You see, I'm the coed with the bad grades and the will to graduate anyway."

"Mmm-hmm. I'm listening."

"Ask me why I came to your office."

For a few moments he was silent, and just when she feared he wouldn't play along, he asked, "What brings you to my office, miss?"

She pressed her body against him. "Dr. Matheson," she said, her New Orleans accent suddenly much heavier. "I just don't know how I'll ever pass your class. I was hoping I could do a little extracurricular work for you."

"What sort of work?"

"Well, Doctor, to be honest, psychology isn't really my best subject." She slid her hand down and gripped his erection. "But I get high marks in physical education."

"Interesting," he said, his voice tight.

"I'd really like to show you my biggest talent, if you'll just have a seat on that desk."

Cole pushed his inbox out of the way and sat down. Juliet kissed him long and deep, letting her hands explore his bare flesh as her body heated up.

When she finished, she flashed him a look of wide-eyed innocence. "Oh, I'm sorry, sir. I just got a little carried away."

He gave her a look. "No apology necessary."

"Then if you don't mind, I'll need you to take your shorts down for me to show you my extracredit work."

"Miss, I hope you understand that there's a strict policy against sexual intercourse between teachers and students here at the university."

"Of course, sir." She donned her best Little-Miss-Innocent face again. "I certainly don't mean to suggest that we have *intercourse*."

"Good."

"But, I can hardly do my extracredit work if you keep your shorts on."

She could see that he was about to protest, so she slid her hand down his chest again to his cock straining through his shorts. She stroked her fingers where it mattered most, and his protest died before he could voice it. He pushed his shorts and briefs down, and she dropped to her knees.

"I'll need to take a few liberties, sir," she said, her mouth only inches from his erection, close enough for him to feel her breath against him.

She hadn't met a guy yet who could resist the promise of a blow job.

"Take all the liberties you need to, miss."

She took his erection in her hand, encased it with her fingers and then her mouth. He was firm and hot against her tongue, and she savored the taste and feel of him.

She licked and teased the head of his cock, stroked his balls with her fingernails, ran her tongue along the length of him until his breath grew ragged and his flesh pulsed in her mouth. Juliet loved the power of having him at her complete mercy, of having control over his pleasure.

Cole gripped the edge of the desk with one hand and buried the fingers of his other hand in her hair as she slowly went from light seductive strokes to an urgent, fast pace that had him straining against her.

She worked him toward the edge, then pushed him over. He spilled himself into her mouth, and she drank him in as he sagged against the desk, gasping and spent. Juliet trailed kisses up his stomach until she reached his mouth, and she silenced his gasps with a kiss as he pulled his shorts back up.

Then he held her against him, buried his face in her hair,

and she felt the satisfaction of a small victory. But it was quickly crowded out by a pang of guilt.

Guilt again, because she'd manipulated him into doing something he hadn't wanted to do, just like last time.

No, she wouldn't allow herself to think that way. This was a game between two adults, and Juliet was here to play and have fun.

She tugged him over to the couch, where she fully intended to continue their little role-playing adventure. This professor-coed thing was pretty fun.

"Juliet," Cole said between kisses. "I hope you don't think this changes my mind."

"Hmm?" She silenced him with a slow, lazy kiss.

He pulled away. "Thanks for *that*," he said, nodding toward the desk, "but I told you up front. We're not having sex tonight."

"You're joking."

"If you want to stay and talk, great. But if you want to do anything more, I can't help you."

Juliet blinked. This was a first for her, and she was nearly stunned silent. She finally said, "You just let me go down on you, knowing you had no intention of finishing what we started?"

"Sorry. I thought you just wanted to make it up to me for the disappearing act."

Anger surged inside of her, and she wanted to hit something.

"Jerk." She shoved him away from her and stood up from the couch.

He stood and followed her out of the room. "You're going to make a lousy research partner if you keep running away."

She turned on him. "Can we just forget this whole stupid research thing? It was a bad idea, and your theory's a weak one at best."

"Absolutely not. You're the one who wanted to do it in the first place. Do you always back out of things when they don't go your way?"

Did she? No, she wasn't a quitter. She just knew when to jump off of a sinking ship.

But then she took in the sight of him again, with his bare chest and his narrow hips and his deliciously well-muscled legs, and she had a hard time imagining him being the sinking ship.

"No, you're right," she said. "I'm not going to back out. But I did ask you for unlimited access...."

"To my bed?" He smiled. "You're right. I'm not playing fair, but this is my theory we're testing. I think I should get to alter the conditions when necessary."

"The problem is, I have a hard time thinking about anything but sex when you're around."

His gaze took on a sensual quality. "You're insatiable."

"Most guys consider that a good quality."

"I wouldn't disagree." He closed the distance between them and took one of her hands in his. "But I'm not going to have sex with you again until I think we're ready."

The anger came back, stronger than before. Juliet jerked her hand away. "Then you can take your half-baked theory to bed with you from now on. Tell me if it keeps you warm at night, okay?"

She didn't wait for his answer. Instead, she stormed down the hallway and straight out the front door, wishing she'd never laid eyes on Cole Matheson.

11

The League of Scandalous Women's Guiding Principle 11:
A scandalous woman is a leader of women. She sets
the example for those who dare to follow.

COLE FELT BAD about the way he and Juliet had left things last night. He'd never intended for her to do what she did, or for him to say what he'd said afterward. But she had, and he had, and he wasn't quite sure why he'd let it all spiral so out of control.

It had taken all his willpower not to stop her from leaving, drag her to his bed and do whatever it took to keep her there. But he also knew that if they didn't spend some time out of bed together, they didn't have a chance.

So after another lousy night's sleep, he'd gotten up early and driven straight to her aunt's old house, hoping she'd be there working so that he could make amends and help. When he pulled into the driveway and saw her car, he heaved a sigh of relief.

He knocked on the front door, and after a few moments passed, she peered through the foyer window at him. He offered a conciliatory smile, but she didn't smile back. He was a little surprised when she opened the door.

"What?" she said as a greeting.

"I'm sorry about last night. I shouldn't have let things go so far."

"So far *down,* you mean?"

He was determined not to laugh, but when she did, he couldn't help it. He held out his hands palms up in an offering of peace. "I'm here to be your servant today. Put me to work."

She raised an eyebrow, but stepped aside so he could enter the house. "My servant? Be careful what you offer."

Cole walked in and looked around. Through the doorway to the living room he could see that furniture had been moved to the center of the room and covered with plastic tarps, and the crown molding had been edged with blue painter's tape.

"You've been busy."

She shrugged.

"Are you going to speak to me, or will I have to grovel some more?"

Groveling made him think of the night before, and Juliet must have had the same thought, because she smiled. "I hope you grovel at least as well as I do."

"Can we call an official truce? I'd like to make last night up to you by helping you with the house."

"I had a different kind of groveling in mind, but okay. I can't turn down manual labor."

"Looks like you're doing great so far." He nodded at the living room that had been prepped for painting.

"The guy at the paint store told me what to do, but I've been afraid to actually crack open a can. And there are so many other projects to do, I feel completely overwhelmed."

"We'll just have to make a plan of attack and get

started.'' Cole looked around at the ancient wallpaper and the worn carpeting. The house was a sizeable project, b—

he knew it was just the kind of thing that would gi—

the chance to work closely together—and wo—

the chance to change Juliet's mind about their re—

She sighed and shrugged. "So what should we — first?"

"Before we paint, we ought to rip down this wallpaper in the foyer and prep the walls. That way we can do all the painting at once."

Juliet nodded. "I've always hated these flowers. It'll be fun to rip it all off."

Cole went out to his trunk and brought back in a box full of tools. They each took a scraper in hand and got to work.

Five minutes later, they'd found at least another five layers of wallpaper below the outermost one, and the prospect of finishing in one day wasn't looking good.

"Have you ever done this before?" Juliet asked as she worked on a loose chunk of paper.

"Not this hard a job, but I have removed wallpaper."

"I'm thinking I'd be better off just selling this place after all."

"I know it's intimidating, but we just have to divide the job into small tasks and complete each one."

"And in the meantime, I still have to run my business and somehow pay the bills," she said as she tore away a two-foot strip.

"And when we're finished, you'll have a beautiful house, a perfect location for your business, and you'll have preserved a piece of your family history."

"Yeah, yeah, yeah. It looks great on paper."

They worked in silence for a while, and Cole realized

that since he'd arrived, he felt rejuvenated. His exhaustion was gone thanks to Juliet. He'd never met a woman who had such a strong effect on him. Maybe it was her energy, or her sex appeal, or her party-girl approach to life, or all of the above. Whatever quality she had that made him feel so alive, he was damn glad she possessed it.

Juliet was some kind of sexy, that was for sure. Tempting, intoxicating, beautiful, wild... She oozed a sex appeal so powerful, resisting was not an option.

"You're in deep thought," she said. "Care to enlighten me?"

Cole pretended to be focused completely on working the wallpaper loose. What if he told her how addicted he'd become to her, how far gone he feared he was? What would she say if he told her she was the most amazing woman he'd ever met and that he couldn't imagine letting her walk out of his life?

She'd freak out. That's what she'd do.

Maybe he could tell her at the same time that he'd lied in order to keep her around, that there was no such thing as the Theory of Sexual Relativity—or at least there hadn't been before he met her. Then he could be sure she'd run for the hills and never look back.

"Sorry, I'm in a daze. I was just thinking about work stuff. Nothing interesting."

"I know I've given you a hard time about it, but I think your work is really interesting. Don't think you'll bore me if you talk about it. I'd love to hear how you first developed your theory about sex."

Uh-oh. Had she read his mind? This was definitely not the turn he'd wanted their conversation to take, especially considering the previous argument about this very topic.

She saw his hesitation and smiled. "It's okay. I promise not to kick you out of the house if you talk about it. I may have overreacted just a tiny bit last night."

"I came up with it recently, when I was watching someone I knew self-destruct with their behavior," he said, scrambling for a coherent answer. No point in mentioning that "someone" was Juliet.

"You mean an old girlfriend?"

"Something like that. It made me realize it was a pattern I'd seen too many times."

"Can you be more specific. Like, exactly how does your theory show that casual sex is bad?"

Good question. "The theory just states what I consider to be a fact. It's our behavior that proves the theory."

She cast him a skeptical glance. "So, let me see if I understand. You and I have great sex, and then we're damaged for life because of it?"

"No, we're damaged by the ensuing emotions that always come along with great sex and that, when ignored, cause trouble."

"What kind of trouble?"

"Let's say that our having sex draws one of us closer, while the other doesn't want to get involved. Then one of us gets hurt."

"Maybe one of us should learn to keep an emotional distance, since one of us seems to be good at erecting a barrier of psychobabble between us anyway."

She said it playfully enough, but Cole still felt the sting of her comment. Did he do that? Was he using psychology to keep Juliet at arm's length? If so, he could only guess it was a self-defense mechanism.

And there he went again, resorting to psychology....

"I think we should agree to disagree for now. Why don't we talk about your work?" he asked, hoping to distract her. "Do you think you'll be overwhelmed with business when you open up the house for parties?"

"It's possible. If we get this place back to its former glory, I can imagine people using it for all kinds of parties, wedding receptions, maybe even weddings."

"The ballroom will be great for that. What did your aunt use that room for?"

"Nothing. It's something my ancestors must have used, but she didn't ever throw parties so big that she needed it."

Cole encountered a particularly stubborn chunk of wallpaper. "Good thing that room's not wallpapered."

"Yeah, it's in the best shape of any room in the house since it was so rarely used."

"So this house has always been in your family?"

"I don't know a lot of details about its history. Ophelia wasn't big on reminiscing about the past, but apparently my great-grandparents built it."

Cole's arm was beginning to go numb, so he switched the scraper to his other hand and leaned against the wall to take a quick break and watch Juliet work.

She was dressed in a pair of old denim overalls that hung loose on her thin frame. Beneath, a tight tank top hugged her breasts and made his thoughts take an erotic turn. She had her long hair pulled back in a ponytail, and she looked irresistibly pretty with her face scrubbed clean of makeup. He loved seeing her like this, so different from her usual seductress self.

"Slacking off already?" she asked, focused on her task still.

He smiled. "Just supervising."

There was a good-sized pile of wallpaper on the floor now, but still plenty more to clear off.

She stopped working and turned to him. "There's no way I could do this whole job alone," she said. "Thank you."

Cole felt an unexpected tightness in his throat and in his chest. In her eyes, he could see his future, or at least what he wanted it to be. Him and her, not just lovers and not just friends, but something more.

More than she wanted now—more than she might ever want.

The question was, how long was he willing to wait?

JULIET PLACED her carefully selected tub of deli-prepared gourmet potato salad on the picnic table and surveyed the rest of the food, relieved not to see any other potato salad and feeling a little ridiculous that she was so worried about bringing the right food to Cole's family get-together.

Even the simple movement of putting down the potato salad reminded her of how hard she'd worked her under-used muscles yesterday. She felt as though she'd been dragged around by an angry mob, kicked and beaten for sport. Juliet definitely needed to start putting in more time at the gym.

Cole, on the other hand, seemed unfazed by the day he'd spent working her like a slave from morning until dark. She could tell he worked out a lot…. Maybe he'd consider being her workout buddy. Or not. She doubted she'd be able to focus much on gym equipment if she had Cole around sweating and looking delicious.

She'd found it impossible to stay angry with him about Friday night, especially when she'd been wrong to try to coerce him into having sex in the first place. The moment she saw him on her doorstep, dressed in his old work clothes and ready to help, her heart had melted. It frightened her a little how happy she'd been to see him, in spite of everything else.

In fact, everything about her feelings toward Cole was getting a little scary. Their conversation yesterday had replayed in her head again and again. It had bothered her for reasons she couldn't quite pinpoint. She had to keep reminding herself that Cole's so-called theory was a load of hooey, and that regardless of how right they might have felt together, they were wrong for each other.

He seemed unwilling to even face the possibility that he related to her more as a psychologist than as a lover, and that, more than any other reason, was why they couldn't be more than lovers or friends.

"I forgot to warn you," Cole said. "My family can be nosy. They might ask you some pretty personal questions."

Juliet turned to him, and over his shoulder she saw that all the adults in the backyard had stopped what they were doing to gawk at them. She enjoyed being the center of attention, but not like this.

"Should I tell them we're only sleeping together to advance scientific knowledge?"

Cole gave her a look. "Tell them whatever you want. Just remember I can exact revenge if you cast me in a bad light."

"Don't I know it. Until the other night, I had no idea you could be so vengeful." She tried to sound serious, but her smile betrayed her.

"I'm full of surprises."

A small blond boy with a blue drink mustache came running up. "Uncle Cole!"

"Hey, Jackson." Cole picked him up and gave him a bear hug, then stood him back on the grass again. "This is my friend, Miss Juliet."

Juliet said hi and smiled.

Jackson produced a huge blue grin. "Is she your *girl*-friend? Mom said you were gonna get married."

Juliet felt her eyes widen, so she rearranged her face back into a neutral expression. "Is there something you're not telling me?"

Cole shrugged. "I warned you." To Jackson he said, "I think your mom was just kidding."

"No, she said you were acting crazy for some lady."

For the first time, Juliet witnessed Cole looking thoroughly embarrassed. "I'll have to have a little talk with your mom."

"Could you tell her that she needs to buy me a new attack helicopter with the machine gun sounds and the remote control?"

"I'll mention it."

"Oh, good, you're here!" Delia said as she came out the back door. She hugged Cole first, then Juliet. "I'm so glad you made it."

Juliet smiled. "I was just meeting Jackson."

"Yeah," Cole said. "Our little nephew was enlightening us about recent family conversations."

Jackson spotted a bird landing on the lawn and took off after it, waving his arms and screeching. Juliet watched, and she realized that children were sorely missing from her life. Not children of her own, but other people's children.

So many of her friends got too busy once they had kids, and she didn't have any family children to borrow.

She looked around at the children laughing and playing in the yard, and she decided Cole was even luckier than she'd first thought. Having kids around made families feel alive and vibrant. She'd always known it with regard to the parties she threw, without being able to articulate it. Parties with children were always the happiest—the messiest too, but that didn't count for much in the face of so much blatant, grinning-ear-to-ear joy.

Delia hurried away to break up a nearby toddler fight over a dump truck, and Cole led Juliet to a set of chaise lounges.

"I would introduce you to everyone, but it might feel like you're being fed to the wolves. We'll just let them come to us—and believe me, they will."

The toddler fight resolved, Delia came back over.

"Where's Max?" Cole asked.

She made a face. "When he found out I was coming to the party, he decided to work."

"Uh-oh. Sounds like the strike isn't working out as planned."

"Not at all." She sank down onto the chaise beside Cole and rested her head on his shoulder. "Which is fine because I don't want to see him anymore, either. Will you hit your brother for me?"

"I'm not sure it'll do much good, but I'd be happy to do it anyway. I talked to him last week, and he was about as receptive to my advice as usual."

"You mean he didn't hear a word you said," Delia said.

"Exactly."

She sighed. "Oh, well, we can just become one of those

bitter old couples who sleep in separate beds and always sit in different rooms.''

Juliet felt for Delia, but she couldn't help thinking this was just a prime example of why she didn't want to settle down and get married. Eventually, even the best of marriages could end up unhappy.

''Why don't I go round up my rug rats and bring them over here to meet you?'' she said to Juliet.

''Sounds great.''

Delia left, and Juliet felt a renewed conviction that she wanted to help her friend repair her marriage.

''I got to know Delia a little better over coffee last week,'' she said to Cole, then glanced around to be sure Delia was out of earshot. ''She told me about their twenty-year anniversary coming up, and I want to throw a party for them.''

''A party is a great idea. But you shouldn't go through the trouble, especially when they're not even speaking to each other—''

''I've already decided I'm going to do it. It's been a long time since I've met someone I immediately liked as much as Delia. I just need some help from you in the planning.''

''Sure, and I'll cover whatever costs are involved, too.''

''That's not necessary,'' Juliet said, though after looking at her budget this week, it would help. Between a recent drop in business and getting her aunt's house into move-in condition, she was nearly broke.

''I insist—no arguments,'' Cole said, and Juliet breathed a silent sigh of relief.

''But of course, we can't very well throw a party for them unless they get over this marriage strike thing first.''

''Yeah.'' Cole shook his head. ''They're really one of

the greatest couples I know. I hate to see them on the outs like this."

An idea came to Juliet, and she nearly giggled at its brilliance. "Remember how I used old photos of you to make that continuous video slide show at your birthday party?"

Cole smiled. "Yeah, that was great."

"What if we could trick them into being together one night? If we could get our hands on their old wedding and honeymoon photos, maybe even a wedding video if they have one, we could force them to sit down and watch it together. It might remind them of why they fell in love in the first place."

"I like it. I think I can get hold of their old photos and wedding video, no problem."

Delia came back out of the house with three kids following behind her. The youngest, a beautiful little blond girl who looked identical to Delia, was followed by the two older kids, who both had Max's darker coloring and piercing blue eyes…much like Cole's.

"Juliet, meet Tyler, Brianna and Katie," Delia said.

She smiled and nodded her way through the greetings, but her mind was elsewhere. She'd been seized with the idea of what Cole's kids might look like—his kids with her, that is.

And her stomach was seized up, horrified by the whole notion. It must have been all the craziness in her life recently, for her hot, carefree fling to turn into such an impossible mess. She owed Rebecca a kick in the shins for planting that what-would-our-kids-look-like notion in her head.

Somehow, some way, she had to untangle herself from Cole, before she ended up a part of his big, boisterous family.

Before she found herself in a life she absolutely did not want.

12

---

*The League of Scandalous Women's Guiding Principle 12:
A scandalous woman never looks back. She learns from
the past, but she keeps her eyes focused on the future.*

EVER SINCE THE FAMILY PICNIC, Juliet had been distant and
weird, in spite of the fact that she and Cole had been working together almost every day on the renovations. In the
past few weeks, they'd managed to paint most of the rooms
in the house, have the carpeting ripped out, the hardwood
floors restored, and the kitchen and bathrooms updated,
while on the outside of the house, the roof had been replaced along with some rotting pieces of wood on the
porch.

They'd made great progress in a really short time, and
yet Juliet didn't seem to be all that happy about it. Whatever her problem was, she needed to loosen up.

They'd spent the morning putting a final coat of red paint
on the ballroom, a daunting task thanks to the size of the
room, but the effort was worth it. The place looked amazing. He never would have chosen red, but Juliet had been
right to think that it was the perfect color. It made the huge
room feel warm, intimate and welcoming, and the crystal
chandeliers that hung from the ceiling cast a warm glow
that only added to the intimacy.

But Cole seemed to be happier that the major work in the house was done than Juliet, and he was determined to get her to relax and stop being so uncharacteristically stiff.

By whatever means necessary.

Cole picked up the paintbrush and dipped it in the red paint. He eyed Juliet's pristine white T-shirt and her old cutoff denim shorts as she was removing painter's tape from the crown moldings. They needed a little decoration. And she needed to loosen up.

With a flick of his wrist, there was a spray of red paint across the front of her outfit and her thigh. She shot him a look of death.

"Why did you do that?" she asked through clenched teeth. It was the first thing she'd said to him in an hour.

Cole shrugged. "Felt like it?"

She glanced down at the bucket of paint, then the dry paintbrush lying next to it.

"Don't even think about it," he said, knowing she'd do the opposite.

She made a move for the paintbrush, and he put himself in her path and caught her in his arms. Once he'd secured her arms, he took his paintbrush and made a nice red stripe across her cheek.

Juliet made a sound something like a growl. "You'll pay for that."

"Do I look scared?"

He let her wiggle out of his grasp, and then she grabbed the plastic cup of paint he'd been using to do the edge work and threw it at him. Red paint splashed across his T-shirt and his bicep. He laughed, causing Juliet to narrow her eyes like a feline on the defensive.

Clearly, she needed even more loosening up. He dipped

his brush in the paint bucket and flicked it at her again, making a haphazard X across her front.

She made another animal sound.

"I think you're going to have to take that off."

"Oh yeah? I'm not getting naked unless you do, too." Then she dived for the paint can again. Before Cole could stop her, she'd hurled what was left in the gallon can at him, and his outfit was oozing red paint.

He looked down at himself, then up at her, and smiled. Paint dripped from his shorts onto his legs and shoes. "I guess I had that coming."

She dropped the bucket, not at all looking relaxed as he'd hoped. "Go ahead. Strip."

"What's going on, Juliet? Lately you've been acting like I ran over your dog, and today you're worse than ever."

"Nothing. Nothing's going on. I just feel bad about you helping me when I can't afford to pay you."

That again? They'd had this conversation already, and he'd tried before to find out why she'd really been so stand-offish lately. He wasn't buying her excuse, but his clothes were continuing to ooze paint onto his legs and shoes. He took off his shirt and started removing his shoes and socks.

"But I've told you, this isn't work to me. This is fun. I wouldn't take payment even if you could afford it."

He could make educated guesses about her problem. She'd bought into her aunt's extreme ideas a little too much, she was afraid of the bond that had developed between them, she thought that to be happy she had to be single... Maybe she was even falling in love with him, the way he'd fallen in love with her.

The way he'd fallen in love with her.

He'd never allowed the reality of it to sink in before, but

it was true. He loved Juliet, and he couldn't imagine his future without her. The realization was both thrilling and terrifying.

Thrilling because knowing what he wanted was the first step toward having it. Terrifying because he knew what he wanted and what she wanted were far from the same things.

A drop of paint fell from his shorts to his bare foot, jarring him back to reality.

"Cole, I think you should leave," Juliet said, her arms crossed over her red-splotched chest.

Definitely not the reaction he'd been going for.

He took off his shorts and stood there in his underwear.

"I can't go anywhere like this," he said, crossing his arms over his chest, too, ready to stand his ground.

"Didn't you bring a change of clothes?" she said, her gaze lingering on his underwear.

He shrugged. "I wasn't planning for you to hurl a bucket of paint at me. Guess I'm stuck here until my clothes dry."

Juliet gave him a calculating look. "You planned this."

"I'm not above a little subversive action to get what I want."

"Which is?"

"You to loosen up. You've been acting like you're the deer and I'm the big bad hunter ever since we went to that family picnic. Is it my family—were they that obnoxious?"

Her cheeks turned a few shades lighter than the streak of red paint on her face. "Not at all, and I haven't been acting like a deer."

He closed the distance between, then took her into his arms. "Are you mad because we haven't had sex in three weeks?"

Truth be told, withholding from her had nearly driven

him crazy, but she hadn't tried to seduce him again since the incident at his house, and his brain had welcomed the chance to get to know her better outside of bed. His body, on the other had had different ideas, and now his brain agreed that the abstinence had gone on long enough.

She punched him in the chest. "If I wanted to have sex with you, we would have had sex."

He considered protesting, but he knew she was right. He couldn't have resisted her for long. "So why did you decide to stop testing out my theory?"

She looked at him for a long moment without saying anything. "Because I was afraid you'd get hurt. From the start, you've taken things too seriously."

Ouch. "Does that mean you agree with me, then?"

He could feel her tense up. "Is that what you want to hear? Yes, Cole, you were right. Casual sex is bad, bad, bad. People get hurt, lives get ruined, blah, blah, blah."

"No, that's not what I want to hear."

She opened her mouth to speak, but he placed a soft kiss on her lips before she could argue any more.

He wanted to believe that if she didn't love him now, or was too afraid to love him, or was too afraid to admit she loved him, it didn't matter. They'd get where they needed to go in time. He wanted to believe that, but he wasn't sure anymore that it was true.

He deepened the kiss when she didn't resist, and after a minute she responded with enthusiasm of her own. Cole let his hands slide under her shirt, up her bare back to her bra strap. He wanted her badly enough not to care about the paint everywhere or the fact that they were both grungy from having worked all day. Unsnapping her bra, he felt himself grow hard, and she had to have felt it, too, but she didn't resist.

Instead, she made a delicious purring sound low in her throat and pressed herself harder against him. He found her earlobe and began to suck it. When he inched his hands up her rib cage to her breasts, then teased her nipples with a feather touch, she sighed and squirmed.

And then she stiffened.

"What's wrong?" Cole whispered.

"We can't do this," she said, pulling away.

"Sure we can. I can even do all the work." To prove his point, he unbuttoned and unzipped her shorts, then slid his fingers beneath her panties. She closed her eyes and sighed. As he massaged the soft, hot flesh between her legs, he could feel her will to resist disappear.

Cole tugged her shorts and panties down, then pinned her against the doorframe—one of the few unpainted surfaces in the room. He wanted her badly enough to take her right then and there, but he wanted just as badly to show her how well he knew her body, how great they were together.

He pinned her with his gaze as he licked his fingers, tasting her, then began to massage her again. She let her head fall back against the doorframe as her breathing grew shallow, as she became so slick, so ready to accept his cock inside her.

He watched pleasure soften her features as he brought her closer to climax, and then he kissed her when he knew she was about to come. He drank in her moans of pleasure as her body convulsed against him, as her muscles contracted at his fingertips.

His own ache had grown until he could hardly stand still,

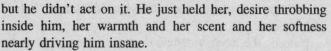

but he didn't act on it. He just held her, desire throbbing inside him, her warmth and her scent and her softness nearly driving him insane.

After a few moments, Juliet pushed at his chest until he stepped back and she could look him in the eye. "Cole, I love our physical relationship, but I don't want to mislead you—"

"Stop," he said, placing a finger on her lips. "I know the deal."

"Do you?" She hesitated, and he got a sick feeling in his gut, as if she was about to deal a deathblow. "Or do you just think that if you keep hanging around long enough, if you keep being the perfect guy, I'll eventually have to fall for you?"

Out of nowhere, his temper flared. He'd been patient, and he wasn't sure how much longer he could continue to be. If Juliet wanted to be alone, sooner or later he'd have to oblige. He wanted to drive himself inside her and make love to her until her will to resist was gone. He needed to go somewhere and calm down.

"I'd better go." He stepped back again, and Juliet looked down at the paint-splattered mess she'd made of him.

He forced his voice to take on a lighter tone than he felt. "I'll just take some newspaper to spread in my car seat to keep it clean."

She grabbed her panties and shorts from the floor and tugged them back on. "I'm sorry, Cole, but—"

"No apology necessary," he said between clenched teeth.

He headed for the foyer, where he'd seen a discarded paper waiting to be recycled. She followed after him.

"Cole, I never meant for things to go this far."

Neither had he, at least not when he'd stumbled into bed with her that first night. But now that he was in love with Juliet, going too far was the least of his problems.

JULIET TAPED UP the last box of office supplies and pushed it to the front door for Finn to carry to the car. Any Occasion had officially closed down its French Quarter location and would open up next week in her aunt's old house. Permission had been granted by the neighborhood association and the city for her to run the business in the mostly residential neighborhood, and now all they had to do was set up an office over the weekend.

Finn came back in and made a face when he saw the size of the final box. "Is this all?"

"That's it," she said, looking around one last time to make sure the place was ready for inspection by the new owner.

As Finn was carrying the box out the door, Juliet's cell phone rang, and she dug it out of her bag. "Hello?"

"Great news, Jule."

It was Rebecca, with that giddy, breathless tone in her voice that she had so often these days.

"What's up?"

"Any chance you can meet me at the bridal shop right now?"

"Um, I was just about to go with Finn over to the house to start setting up our office."

"Do you think he'd mind working alone for a little while?"

"I don't know. Why?" Juliet asked, not sure she wanted to hear the answer.

"We've moved up the wedding date!" Rebecca nearly squealed.

Juliet hadn't heard her so excited since she'd discovered sour apple martinis. "To when?" she asked as her stomach twisted into a knot.

"Don't hate me. We want to do it around late October, in four more weeks. Do you think it's possible?"

Finn came back into the building, and she gave him a look of wide-eyed panic. He mouthed, "What?" and she held up a finger telling him to wait.

Juliet forced herself to sound light and unfazed. "Anything's possible. You just won't have time to worry over the details—no being wishy-washy about choosing flowers or dresses or anything else."

"That stuff's not important anyway," Rebecca said. "But that's why I was hoping you could meet me now, so we can hurry and get the dresses picked out."

Juliet glanced at her watch. "I guess I could be there in about an hour. I have to do a walk-through inspection with the owner of this building, and then I could come."

"Perfect! I'll get there first and start narrowing down my choices, so just come whenever you finish up there."

When Juliet hung up the phone and shoved it back in her bag, Finn gave her an impatient look.

"That was Rebecca," she said. "I have to go help her pick out dresses for her wedding."

"You're leaving me to do all the dirty work again?"

"I'm sorry. She sounds like she's on the verge of buying every dress in the store."

"You'd better go then, lest you end up marching down the aisle in a bubblegum pink ruffled thing with a gigantic bow on your butt."

"My thoughts exactly."

The new owner of the building arrived, and they did the inspection without incident. Five minutes later, Juliet had handed over the keys, feeling not even an ounce of regret. She wouldn't miss the shabby little building, and although she wouldn't have believed it a month ago, she was excited about opening up the business in the family house.

She and Finn were standing outside the building when Cole pulled up in his car. She'd hoped to avoid him today, and yet the sight of him gave her a thrill. They hadn't seen each other since the painting incident, and Juliet had felt out of sorts and confused ever since. Then when Cole had called last night to say he'd stop by and help her and Finn move boxes, she'd tried to turn down his help, but he'd insisted.

Finn made a little "ahem" sound in his throat and raised an eyebrow at Juliet.

"I thought you were calling it quits," he whispered when she didn't respond.

Cole got out of the car and headed toward them.

"He's persistent," she whispered back before turning to Cole.

"Hey, am I too late to help?" he asked.

"Unfortunately, I have to run off to help Rebecca with some wedding stuff," she said, partly relieved to have an escape. "Finn's about to head over to the house alone to start setting up."

Cole's gaze warmed her from the inside out. She'd felt awful about the way he'd left the other day, and part of her had wanted to go chasing after him and have wild, sweaty paint-splattered sex all night long. But her conscience had held her back. Their relationship had taken on a note of seriousness that she didn't want—that she'd tried her best to avoid from the start—and she knew it would only get worse if she didn't put a stop to it.

But Cole was so damned sexy, smart, fun…. So damned perfect, she was powerless to send him away for good. In fact, seeing him now, she was suddenly tempted to call Rebecca back and cancel.

That would have been giving in to a weakness that would only get her in trouble.

"I can help you unload boxes, if you want," Cole offered to Finn.

Finn beamed. "I'd love it."

He was clearly angling for the opportunity to pry information out of Cole.

"Well," Juliet said, reluctant to leave the guys alone. "I guess I'll get going."

Finn smiled. "Don't worry about us. We'll be sure not to strain any important muscles."

Fifteen minutes later, Juliet was inside the bridal shop, being ushered into a dressing room with Rebecca. Once they were alone with Rebecca's selection of dresses, she eyed her friend and asked, "Okay, so why the sudden rush to get married? Please don't tell me you're pregnant."

Rebecca laughed. "Of course not. We just can't deal with this long-distance romance thing. It sucks to have Alec all the way in San Diego."

She undressed as she talked, then tried on the first dress, a long white fitted one with beaded fringe that reminded Juliet of flapper girls. Juliet helped her zip it up.

"So what? He's packing up and moving to New Orleans in the next couple of weeks?"

"Yep, he's breaking his apartment lease and moving

here. It's great that he's a freelance journalist, so he doesn't have to worry about changing jobs.''

"Yeah, that's great,'' Juliet said without much feeling.

Rebecca turned around and examined herself in the mirror. "You'd better start sounding happy for me or I'll pick out a *really* hideous bridesmaid dress for you to wear.''

"I want to be a flapper girl. I think you should buy that dress so I can get a matching maid of honor one in red.''

"Ooh, I like the sound of that.'' Rebecca thought about it for a few seconds. "That's it!''

"What?''

"We'll do a whole Roaring Twenties theme for the wedding—it'll be great.''

It did sound pretty cool. "If you keep making your decisions at this rate, we can have the wedding planned by next weekend.''

"Don't tempt me,'' Rebecca said, admiring herself from all angles. "If I don't start getting regularly laid again soon, I may lose my freaking mind.''

"I can imagine.'' Juliet looked through the rack of bridesmaid dresses to see if any of them fit the bill for a Roaring Twenties–themed wedding.

"I didn't see any dresses out there that would match the style of this one,'' Rebecca said.

"Finn knows an incredible costume maker. I wonder if we could hire him to make the dresses we want.''

Rebecca looked at her like she'd lost it. "You want to hire a costume maker to design my bridesmaid dresses?''

"He makes costumes as in drag queen wear. It's not always easy for those guys to find fabulous evening gowns in a size 34 long.''

"You think he'd be willing?''

"I think Finn could persuade him on our behalves. He's got some pretty convincing methods, I hear."

"Finn is so hot—I've always thought it was a waste he doesn't go for girls."

"Yeah, well, now you've got your own hottie, so you don't need to worry about Finn."

Juliet dug around in her bag until she found her calendar, made a note on it to talk to the costume maker about the dresses, and then looked at her schedule for the next week.

"I can meet up with you again Wednesday at the florist if you want to pick out flowers then. I'll need some time to research twenties decorating before we can pick out decorations."

Rebecca was admiring herself in the mirror again, clearly pleased with her choice of dresses. "Sounds good." She turned to Juliet. "I can't tell you how much I appreciate your helping me plan the wedding. I'd be clueless without you."

Juliet waved away her thanks. "That's what friends are for."

"Yeah, but you don't exactly approve of my rush to get married, and you've managed to help me without criticizing once."

"I do so approve!" Juliet lied, feeling ridiculous even as she said it.

Rebecca eyed her skeptically but said nothing.

"I've just been feeling a little sorry for myself, that's all."

"Are you still worried about going out partying alone?"

"No, I've got Finn. He's not married yet."

Rebecca got a wistful look for a moment. "And he can take you to all the cool gay nightclubs."

"Yeah, that's why I want to stay single. Gay nightclubs."

"You know what I mean. It's nice to go out dancing occasionally without feeling like fresh meat dangling in front of the wolves."

She had a point.

"What about Cole? Are you guys still just doing the nasty, or is it getting serious?"

"He's just helping me renovate the house—that's all," she said, nearly blushing at the thought of their diversion from renovations last weekend.

"Please. You can't expect me to buy that. Guys don't just do manual labor without the expectation of a little lovin' in return."

"He's not like that."

"Every guy is like that," Rebecca said.

"Cole's different." Confounding, confusing and sexy as hell. He left her head spinning, and he made her crazy with all his talk of theories and emotional damage, but he was also one of the nicest guys she'd ever met.

"If you say so. I guess I'm not gonna convince you to have a double wedding or anything."

"You promise you'll still go out with me occasionally? Even after you're an old married woman?"

Rebecca smiled and gave her a hug. "Till we're old and gray, babe."

Till they were old and gray? Did she want to be out partying in her orthopedic shoes?

No, she didn't, she realized for the first time.

But somehow, without trying, she'd managed to convince everyone in her life who cared that she did.

13

The League of Scandalous Women's Guiding Principle 13:
A scandalous woman takes what she wants when it
can't be had by more subtle means.

COLE LISTENED to Finn talk as they unpacked boxes, aware that he was subject to some serious pro-Juliet propaganda. Not that he minded. He actually thought it was great that she had such a loyal friend. Finn had spent most of the past hour talking about what a talented, smart, amazing woman Juliet was, and Cole had kept his mouth shut. He already knew Juliet inside and out, but it was interesting to hear someone else's view of her.

He suspected Finn was just trying to loosen him up so he could start fishing for information himself. After all, what good friend wouldn't want to dig for dirt on a lover? His suspicions were confirmed when Finn asked in an overly casual tone, "So, what are your intentions with Juliet?"

"My intentions?" Cole smiled, suddenly feeling as if he was being interviewed by a protective father.

"Are you serious about her?"

"I'm serious, she's not."

Finn was removing party supply catalogs from a box and

artfully arranging them on the coffee table. "I think our Juliet has issues, if you know what I mean."

"I do." Cole leaned against the desk, unable to help without knowing where things were supposed to go. He crossed his arms over his chest.

"But that doesn't mean she can't be won over. She just needs the right guy to do it."

Cole had been sure he was that guy, but he was beginning to doubt it. Except for today, they hadn't spoken since the paint incident, and he knew if he'd left it up to her, they probably wouldn't ever speak again.

Instead of growing closer, he and Juliet seemed to be growing apart. She was doing everything she could to avoid him, and he couldn't do much to win her over if she was determined not to be won.

Finn turned to him. "I might be stepping over the line here, but I'm usually a pretty good judge of these things, and I think you're the one for her. Don't give up, okay?"

Cole nodded, feeling a little odd having a heart-to-heart with a guy he barely knew. "I'm not out of the game yet."

The front door opened, and in walked the subject of their conversation.

"Hey, guys," she said, smiling as if she had a pretty good hunch what they'd been talking about.

"Hey, Jule," Finn said, suddenly Mr. Innocent. "I was just about to leave." He glanced at his watch. "I've got a dinner date."

"Thanks for helping tonight," she said. "The bridal shopping expedition was a success, but I may need your help with something else."

"I can come back over tomorrow if you want some more help unpacking."

"Thanks, but I mean with Rebecca's wedding. Do you think you could talk your dressmaker friend into doing some bridesmaid dresses?"

Finn shrugged. "He'd probably do it for the right price. But he has a strict policy against making ugly dresses."

"Rebecca wants a Roaring Twenties theme for her wedding. We're thinking red, beads, tassels—something to-die-for."

"Sounds fabulous. I'll talk to him."

"Thanks, Finn. I owe you big-time."

Once they'd said goodbye and Finn left the house, Juliet turned to Cole and sighed. "I hope he didn't grill you too much."

"He was just looking out for your best interests."

"I can imagine."

Cole was unprepared for how wound up he was now that they were finally alone. He felt like a coil, ready to spring at any moment, ready to take Juliet into his arms and carry her back out into her secret garden, where he'd do his damnedest to erase all her reservations about him.

Not that her reservations were totally unwarranted. If he had the guts, he'd tell her his theory had just been an excuse to get closer to her. He'd face the consequences of his actions and trust that if they were meant to be together, everything would work out.

So why couldn't he? And why couldn't he just tell her he loved her and let her deal with it. If she was really the woman for him, she wouldn't run away from his feelings.

Every time he tried to tell her the truth, his throat seized, or they got into an argument, or Juliet did something to completely distract him from conversation. His excuses sounded flimsy even to him, yet when he looked at her now, he couldn't summon the will to tell her.

"What's up?" she asked. "You look like you're having deep thoughts again."

Here was the perfect opportunity. Handed to him on a silver platter... All he had to do was open his mouth and tell the truth. "I was just thinking..."

"Oh, my God, I can't believe you guys found this!" Juliet picked up a raggedy looking voodoo doll, like the ones sold in tourist shops all over the city, from the desk. "This is Francois, my good-luck doll."

And then stuff like this happened.

"Francois was lost?"

"I haven't seen him in months." She was still marveling at the doll.

"I think I saw Finn pull that thing out of a file cabinet."

"Ah, that explains it. Neither of us are much on filing. He must have fallen in and gotten lost."

She placed the doll carefully next to her computer monitor, and Cole reminded himself that the window of opportunity was still open. He could still tell her.

"Juliet, we need to talk."

She turned to him, her hair cascading over her shoulder the same way it did over his pillow. "You're right, we do. I owe you my undying gratitude for helping so much lately, with the house, with the move today, and I'm sorry I've been a little distant—"

"That's not what I meant."

A look of panic crossed her eyes, if he wasn't mistaken. "Don't get heavy on me, okay? I'm stressed out, and I may not be behaving as nicely as I should."

"Juliet—"

"I'm trying to close my aunt's estate, get the house ready, move the business here, keep up with my clients and their parties, help Rebecca plan her wedding… And I guess I just don't know what to do with our relationship."

"I've got some ideas," he said.

She flashed a mischievous grin, ignoring his comment. "We should ask Francois. He knows all the answers."

"Your lucky voodoo doll also offers advice?"

"He's multitalented." Juliet picked up the doll and turned it to face her. "Francois, I'm sorry you spent the past six months locked in a file cabinet. Will you forgive me?"

She looked up at Cole. "He says he isn't sure yet." To the doll she said, "Do you think you could give me some advice?"

Cole watched his chance to have a serious discussion slipping through his fingers.

"He says he'll listen to our problem, but he can't guarantee he'll have an answer." She looked at the doll again. "Cole and I can't seem to agree about sex. I think we should only have it if we keep it casual, and he thinks that's impossible."

Cole took her hand and pulled her closer, then slid his hands around her waist to keep her there. "Would you stop fighting this?"

"I'm not fighting anything. I'm just being realistic."

"Thinking we can keep doing what we have been without negative consequences isn't realistic."

Juliet shot him a look of death and wriggled out of his grasp. "You're right, since you're incapable of lightening up and having a good time. I'm sorry I overestimated you."

This sure as hell wasn't going the way he'd planned.

"Maybe we'd better stop right here, before either of us says something we might regret later."

"Do you always stay so damn calm? Don't you ever just lose it?"

Oh, yeah, he'd lost it the moment he met Juliet. Every decision he'd made since then hadn't made an ounce of sense. "Would it make you feel better if I did?"

"Stop with the psychology, okay? I want you to act like a regular guy having an argument with his girlfriend, not like Dr. Cole Matheson…" She seemed to have realized her slip.

Cole was still reeling from it himself. *Girlfriend?* That was the closest she'd come to admitting they were more than lovers, and the sudden ache in his chest made him realize how much he'd been hoping she'd come around.

"I didn't mean to suggest that I *am* your girlfriend. I just meant—"

"You'd like me to behave as if you are?"

"No!" Her complexion took on a rosy hue. "I just want you to act like a guy and not a psychologist."

"I can't be both?"

"See what I mean? Instead of arguing with me, you keep asking me these irritating questions. Regular guys don't do that!"

Questions came as naturally to him as breathing. "I can see how the questions might get irritating if you don't want to have your actions examined."

"Look, I know I said I'd participate in your study, but I don't think this is going to work. Can't you just find someone else to drive insane?"

This was his chance to come clean. Right here, right now, and she was already angry, so it wouldn't ruin the mood. But it would also seal their fate. No way would she ever want to see him again.

He couldn't live with that. "No, I can't. I want *you*," he said as he closed the distance between them, then covered her mouth with his.

When all else fails, his brother Max always said, shut her up with a kiss. For once, he was taking Max's advice. It hadn't worked last weekend, but maybe it would work today.

And even if it didn't, at least he was kissing her. He'd been longing—aching—for some intimate contact with her all week.

Juliet stiffened at his touch, but she allowed him to keep kissing her. He explored her with his tongue, and soon she melted into him. She snaked her arms around his neck and channeled all her anger into one hungry, desperate, toe-curling kiss. Cole immediately understood the peril of Max's method, because now he couldn't just kiss her.

He wanted more.

But he couldn't ask for more. Not now. This had to be a simple kiss, an embrace, and that was it.

Cole forced himself to pull away, but he kept holding on to her. She fit perfectly in his arms. It was where she belonged, even if she didn't realize it yet.

It was where he wanted to keep her, if only he could figure out how.

"We've got to stop doing that," she said. "It always gets us in trouble."

She was right about the trouble part, anyway. Cole willed himself not to want her so badly, but it didn't work. There was no way he could stop wanting her.

"Maybe if I think about paying taxes," he said.

Juliet smiled. "It works for me."

"Problem is, when I try to picture my tax forms, I end up picturing you lying naked on top of them."

"Hmm, that is a problem." She took his hands from around her waist and held them in hers. "Now that we know casual sex just doesn't work between us, can we at least be friends?"

Cole felt as if she'd punched him in the gut. He started to make a smart-ass comment about her using the most dreaded of all brush-offs, but he stopped himself. If he couldn't have her the way he wanted her now, then yeah, he did want to at least be friends.

He summoned all his willpower to produce a smile, though it felt like a weary one. "Friends, huh?"

"Real friends. I'm not just saying it. I'd miss you from my life."

"I think I can handle that," he said, though he wasn't sure if he could handle it for more than a day or two.

He needed time to think, to plan his words and his actions.

She smiled her smile that could lead ships to shore. "Good. I've been thinking about Delia and Max. Any word on whether they're over the marriage strike?"

"No, I dropped by yesterday to sneak their photos and the video out, and they were still fighting. The stuff is in my car, by the way."

"Thanks for getting it all. I'll go ahead and prep our little presentation for them, if you can figure out a way to get Max here on Friday night. I'll make sure Delia shows up."

"The anniversary party is Saturday, isn't it?"

"Yep, so if we can't get them back together Friday night,

it should make for an interesting party." Juliet let go of his hands and clapped hers together. "But we won't worry about that, because our private reunion party's going to work."

Cole smiled at her enthusiasm. Yeah, he wanted her as a friend, because she was the brightest spot in his life. And he wanted her as so much more than that.

MAX WAS SITTING on the parlor sofa with Cole, demanding to know where the big-screen TV was and why they weren't watching the game Cole had apparently lured him there with the promise of. If Delia didn't get there in the next few minutes, their plan might be blown, and even if she did get there in time, Juliet still couldn't be sure one or both of them wouldn't march right out the door when they saw the other.

Juliet had spent the past two days working her butt off to get everything ready for Max and Delia's anniversary party tomorrow night, and if they didn't get back together willingly by the end of the night tonight, she'd be tempted to lock them in the bedroom and not let them out until they'd made up.

As she had watched their wedding video and videotaped their old photos to create a video slide show, even she had gotten a little teary-eyed. In spite of her recent feelings that their marriage troubles were reason enough for her to avoid serious relationships, she couldn't help but see all the good in their marriage, too.

She'd been right about them in the first place. They were one of the few great examples of marriage that she'd ever seen, and with all her heart she wanted to see them happy together again.

The doorbell rang, and Juliet cast a nervous glance at Cole before opening the door and greeting Delia.

"I've got a little surprise for you," Juliet said, right before Delia spotted Max sitting in the living room on the sofa.

"Him? I'm leaving," Delia declared, turning back toward the door.

"What's she doing here?" Max said. "If there's no big-screen TV and no game, I'm gonna kick your ass, little brother."

Juliet caught Delia's arm as she made a move back out the door. "Please, just give us five minutes. If you still want to leave then, I won't try to stop you."

Delia cast a suspicious look at her but said nothing. Juliet closed the door behind her and breathed a little sigh of relief that they'd overcome one small hurdle.

"What's this all about?" Max said.

Juliet smiled her most diplomatic smile. "I'll need both of you to sit down on the couch."

They both looked at her as if she was crazy, and Cole flipped on the small television that in no way could be classified as "big-screen." Delia sat at the opposite end of the couch from Max, on the edge with her back stiff.

A part of Juliet really loved knowing that somewhere out there, a couple could be married for twenty years and still be deeply in love. And she knew they were. They'd just hit a rough patch of road. A really rough patch, judging by the tension that was palpable in the air between them.

It was her job to smooth the way again.

She'd never considered herself a romantic person. Sure, she loved the trappings of romance, but somehow the sentiment of it had never interested her much. And yet, something about Max and Delia's relationship tugged at her heartstrings.

"Max and Delia, this is your life together." Juliet pressed Play on the VCR, and an image of their wedding ceremony appeared on the TV screen.

"You're not going to make us watch this damn wedding video, are you?" Max asked.

Delia shot him a pointed look. "I know what torture that would be for you, right?"

Juliet had anticipated some resistance. She hit the pause button. "You two stop it. I don't want to hear any more arguing. Consider this a little walk down memory lane. If, after you've watched your own wedding, you still feel like scratching each other's eyes out, go ahead."

Max looked at Cole. "Were you in on this?"

Cole shrugged and smiled. "I may have helped a little."

Max rolled his eyes and turned back to the TV. "Go ahead, let's get this over with."

She hit the play button again, and they watched as the wedding ceremony went through all the traditional motions. Delia had been a beautiful bride, Juliet thought, so incredibly young. Her eyes were full of excitement and nervousness and absolute adoration when she looked at Max.

And when Max looked at her, it was easy to see how their marriage had lasted twenty years. The two clearly adored each other equally, even if they'd spent the past month at complete odds.

Juliet squirmed at the pang in her chest. Had a guy ever looked at her with such adoration? Probably not.

But that was okay, because with adoration came a whole slew of complications she didn't have to deal with in her uncomplicated life.

Then she caught sight of Cole, age ten, and her heart melted. He had been an usher in the wedding, and in his black tuxedo, he looked so grown-up and yet so young, just a suggestion of the man he was to become. She glanced over at him perched on the arm of a high-backed chair, and then quickly looked away again, uncomfortable with what he might have seen in her eyes. Just sexual attraction really, for the completely grown-up man he was, but she was afraid it might have looked like something more.

The wedding ceremony came to a close, and the video switched abruptly to the reception, where the bride and groom were having their first dance as husband and wife. Guests were gathered at tables around the dance floor, looking on and smiling, while young Max and Delia saw no one but each other. There was that mutual look of adoration again.

Juliet felt someone watching her, and she looked away from the TV to see that it was Cole. He was smiling a half smile that made him look as though he had a dirty little secret. He nodded down at Delia and Max, who'd finally stopped looking as if they were about to rush out the door and were riveted to the video. They'd even managed to relax enough to look happy, as if they were both recalling the way they'd felt that day twenty years ago. Cole mouthed the words "let's get out of here," and Juliet agreed; they were only getting in the way.

She stood up and went as quietly as possible to the kitchen, and a few moments later Cole followed. Once the kitchen door was closed, she said, "I think it's working."

"They're not trying to strangle each other. That's a good sign."

"I think once we make them look at the photos on video, they'll be back together for good."

Cole went to her at the kitchen counter and placed his hands on her hips. Definitely not a we're-just-friends gesture. Juliet should have brushed his hands away, but she couldn't.

"You did a great job with this, you know. Thank you for helping my brother and Delia."

"No thanks needed. Delia is my friend, and I want to see her happy."

She tried to ignore the growing warmth in her body his nearness created, tried not to think about what she'd like to be doing on the kitchen counter at that moment.

"Even though you don't believe married people can really be happy?"

There he was again, trying to catch her in a contradiction. "I never said *all* married people couldn't be happy."

"Just you, right?"

"Me and all the millions of people who get divorced."

He traced his finger along her jaw line. "You're such an optimist."

"It's good for my health," she joked. Strange that she *had* managed to be an optimist about almost everything—except her love life.

Being alone with Cole, having him so close, was a dangerous proposition. Not an optimistic thought, but an accurate one. She'd done her best to put distance between them, and nothing seemed to have worked.

In the next room, the sound of the wedding video disappeared, signaling the end of the tape. "We'd better get back out there before they have a chance to start arguing again,'' she said to Cole, thankful for the escape from being alone with him.

''Yeah,'' he said, staring at her mouth. ''We'd better go.''

She slipped away from him and fled out the kitchen door. In the living room, Delia and Max were still sitting a few feet apart on the sofa, staring at the blank blue TV screen.

''For the next event of the evening,'' Juliet said, ''I've prepared a special video for you.''

She went to the TV and removed the wedding tape, then put the photo video she'd made into the VCR. She'd originally thought it could be a surprise for the anniversary party, but in the face of there possibly not being an anniversary party at all, she figured she'd better pull out all the stops to get Delia and Max back together.

While the tape was cueing up, she turned to face the couple and found them both looking a little uncomfortable. That was better than looking murderous. Progress had been made.

The photo montage began to roll, set to a love song Delia had told Juliet was her and Max's song. Images flashed slowly on the screen, starting with their dating days and progressing through their marriage and honeymoon. Next came their early years as young parents, family vacations, parties and picnics at the park. From the outside looking in, Delia and Max's life appeared perfect.

Perfect for someone who wanted that kind of life, Juliet quickly reminded herself. She, on the other hand, was destined to have a different kind of happiness, the same kind her aunt had had. She'd grow old gracefully, hang out with her league of scandalous women and find new ways to raise eyebrows in New Orleans—if such a feat was still possible.

But suddenly there was a hollow feeling in her gut. Max and Delia's life, so full of family and love and happiness, made the existence she foresaw seem a little…empty. For a moment she allowed herself to picture her own photo montage, with Cole as her partner. Their wedding, their honeymoon, their kids, their happiness.

Maybe, just maybe, she could live that kind of life and be happy.

She felt someone's gaze on her again, and she looked over to see Delia watching her. Juliet's cheeks burned as she imagined anyone might have read her mind a moment ago. But then Delia smiled and looked back at the TV.

The photo montage was about to end, and Juliet sensed that the best thing she and Cole could do to help at the moment would be to disappear again. She caught his eye and nodded toward the kitchen, and they both left again.

Once inside the privacy of the kitchen, Cole asked, "Do you think it's working?"

"It's even got me feeling soft-hearted, so I think it has to be working on them."

"You? Feeling soft-hearted?"

She smiled. "Maybe a little."

Cole's eyebrow arched. "Maybe I should be taking advantage of you now, while I can."

Juliet could think of all kinds of ways she'd like to be taken advantage of. "Maybe you should."

On foolish impulse, she went to him and slid her hands up his chest and around his neck, then placed a soft kiss on his lips.

"That didn't feel like a friendly kiss," he said.

Juliet smiled and rested her head on his shoulder, not

sure what she was trying to accomplish but aware that whatever it was, it might lead to her own ruin.

"Do you think they'll notice if we disappear upstairs for a while?" he asked, his breath tickling her cheek.

"I think we need to make sure they're getting along again, and then we can kick them out of here."

"Sounds like a plan."

Juliet peeked through the door and spotted Delia and Max sitting next to each other on the couch. Max had his arm around her, holding her close, and they were talking softly. Juliet imagined apologies being made. And then they kissed, and her heart melted.

She closed the door and turned to Cole with a giddy smile. "Victory."

"Great job," he said and hugged her.

Fifteen minutes later, they'd shuffled Delia and Max out the door, and Juliet felt ridiculously happy for having seen an end to Delia's marriage strike. She collapsed on the sofa and sighed a contented sigh.

Cole sank down next to her and pulled her feet onto his lap. When he began carefully massaging her left foot, she knew for sure he was a near-perfect man—not only was he intelligent, gorgeous, a great lover and a devoted friend, but he also had extremely talented hands.

No, she had to remind herself, he was far from perfect. He might have had a lot of great qualities, but he also hid behind his psychology degree, used psychobabble as a defense mechanism and considered her someone who was emotionally damaged—someone who needed fixing.

But still, he had incredible hands.

"You're looking pretty satisfied with yourself. Want to talk about it?" he asked.

"It's been a successful day, that's all. And I'm looking forward to throwing the first party here tomorrow night."

"How do you like living here in your aunt's house again?"

"It's strange. And wonderful. I feel like she's with me here."

"Maybe she is."

Juliet closed her eyes and focused on Cole's hands, which had moved from her feet to her ankles and calves. She loved her aunt, but there were other things she'd much rather think about at the moment.

Namely, dragging Cole upstairs to her bedroom.

Maybe it was a stupid impulse—okay, it was definitely a stupid impulse—but after all her hard work, she felt as though she deserved to have one last night of sex with Cole. To hell with their plan to just be friends. Friends could have an occasional night of hot sex, couldn't they?

She sent her foot on an expedition across his lap to the bulge in his pants. "I was hoping you were the only person here with me tonight."

"Oh, yeah?"

"I finally got my bedroom all put together. Want to see it?"

He let his hands travel up to her thighs. "There's an invitation I can't refuse."

Something about his tone seemed a little off. "You don't sound all that excited."

"There's something we need to talk about first."

"Let's have fun first and talk later." She crawled onto his lap and nipped at his ear, eager to put everything else out of her mind.

After being deprived of Cole's talents in bed for all this

time, she needed him. She ached for him, and she was going to go crazy if she couldn't have him right now.

"Juliet, really—" He started to protest, but she covered his mouth with hers and kissed him with all the longing she had pent up inside.

The effect was just what she'd hoped. He had to have felt it, too—the crazy ache that had built up between them—because he pulled her against him and returned her intensity with his own.

As they kissed, they scrambled to strip each other of their clothes, and when she finally had Cole naked against her, Juliet felt jittery with desire. She couldn't hold still, couldn't rest until he was inside her, easing that ache.

Somehow they ended up on the floor, on one of Ophelia's Persian rugs, and Juliet couldn't imagine a better use for the old work of art than as a cushion for their lovemaking. She wrapped her legs around Cole and he slid into her in one easy thrust.

She was wet and throbbing for him, and the sensation of him inside her was more intense and delicious than it had ever been before. It took her only a few moments to realize that in their desperation, they'd forgotten about protection.

Cole's eyes were glazed with desire as he looked at her, as he moved inside her, and she knew he was too far gone to realize the mistake they'd made.

She should have stopped them then. But she wanted him in that desperate, reckless way that was beyond thinking. It was stupid, incredibly stupid, and she was having a hard time caring.

Cole thrust into her, his body so tense that he was all hard muscle and perspiration. She could only cling to him, kiss him, take him in, until they were both lost in the rhythm of their lovemaking.

He cradled the back of her head and kissed her long and deep when their climax came. It was simultaneous, explosive, rocking them and forcing them to cry out with the relief of it.

Juliet closed her eyes, unable to look at the intensity in Cole's, unable to face whatever else she might see there. She kissed his neck, his shoulder, his earlobe as the final quakes of her orgasm passed.

Instead of collapsing on top of her, Cole wrapped his arms around her and rolled onto his back, taking her with him. There they rested until they were both coherent again.

"That was intense," Cole finally said, then placed a soft kiss on her forehead.

"Do you know why?"

"I've got some idea," he said. But he didn't.

"We didn't use protection."

Cole tensed again. "Oh, God. I'm sorry. I got so caught up in—"

"Don't apologize. It's as much my fault as yours. I realized pretty early, but I couldn't stop."

Cole sighed. "I've always been very careful. I was clean on my last checkup."

"I've been careful, too. That's the first time I've ever made such a huge mistake."

"Is there any possibility that you could get pregnant?"

"Anything's possible, but I'm taking birth control pills, thank God."

Cole squeezed her tighter against him. "There's never going to be a right time for me to say what I need to tell you," he said.

Juliet closed her eyes, wishing he wouldn't spoil their fun. "Why do I get the feeling I'm not going to like this?" she said, trying to keep her voice light.

"Because you won't. I lied to you about something."

She lifted her head and smiled at him, intent on lightening his mood. "If you're talking about all those nights you faked it in bed, don't worry, I already know."

When he didn't smile back, she knew whatever he was talking about, it was serious.

"Remember how I said I'd created the Theory of Sexual Relativity?"

"I'd have a hard time forgetting that."

"I just made it up to keep you around."

Juliet blinked, processing the information. Okay, she wouldn't have guessed he was capable of such duplicity.

"Because you knew I wouldn't have stuck around otherwise."

"Exactly. And I'm sorry I lied, but I'm not sorry it gave us a chance to get to know each other."

She didn't like being manipulated, and she had a vague sense she'd been played for a fool. It occurred to her now just how ridiculous something called the Theory of Sexual Relativity sounded. And why would an organizational psychologist be formulating sexual theories, anyway?

"Juliet?"

She wasn't sure what to say. "Okay…you lied. Thanks for telling me."

"That's not all," he said.

"If your name's not really Cole, I'm going to be pissed."

He urged her up to a sitting position and took her hands in his. "I'd love nothing more than to go upstairs and make love to you all night, but there's one more thing you have to know before we can do this again."

"Okay, so spill it," she said, growing impatient, not sure she wanted to hear what he had to say.

"All this time we've spent together—there's no way I could keep it casual. I knew from the start that I was falling in love with you."

His gaze pierced her, opened her up and made her feel as if she was bleeding. She tried to squirm away from him, but he held on.

Falling in love with you.

That was exactly the disaster she'd wanted to avoid. Anger came bubbling up inside her, but she didn't want to say something that would hurt him more than the truth—that she couldn't love him back.

His constant psychobabble, his lying to keep her around—it was all too much.

She blinked at the burning in her eyes. "I don't know what to say."

"Say you'll give us a real chance. Say you'll give up the crazy notion that you have to be totally free to be happy."

The anger came bursting forth then. "Our whole relationship is based on a lie. I can't believe you—a psychologist, no less—would think that's okay!"

"I don't think it's okay. That's why I'm telling you now. I'm sorry I didn't say something sooner, but this was the first time I really felt sure you weren't ready to bolt at any moment."

So he'd sensed her softening toward him. Of course he did, ever-perceptive guy that he was. Too bad he couldn't perceive just how much she hated being lied to by a lover.

Juliet stood up from the couch and glared at Cole. "You were sleeping with me under false pretenses."

He stood up, too, and tried to come closer, but she backed away. "I apologize."

"Go to hell," she blurted, surprised by her own fury.

"Juliet—"

"I want you out of my house." She pointed at the door and gave him a look that made it clear she was finished talking.

Cole's expression darkened, but he stood up and got dressed. Juliet snatched her own clothes off the floor and tugged them on.

"I'll call you later. We need to continue this conversation when we're both calm."

"If you call, I won't answer. This conversation is finished, and so are we."

Cole cast a dark look at her, but he went to the door. Before he left, he cast one more glance in her direction. "I'll give you some time to cool off, but I won't leave things like this for long."

"Out!" she yelled.

When he disappeared into the foyer and she heard the front door open and close, she collapsed onto the sofa again. Why was it that her love life had turned serious even when she'd tried her best to keep it anything but?

The reason didn't matter. What mattered was that she'd been right all along. Serious relationships only created serious problems for all involved. And she'd had enough of serious to last her a lifetime.

14

The League of Scandalous Women's Guiding Principle 14: A scandalous woman has control of her emotions at all times. She does not allow her emotions to control her.

DELIA WATCHED from the passenger seat as Max made a wrong turn, away from their neighborhood instead of toward it. Their Suburban lumbered along the dark street, passing other cars headed out for an evening on the town.

"Where are we going?" she asked.

"It's a surprise."

Max was known for many things, but surprising his wife wasn't one of them. "If you're thinking of stopping at the 7-Eleven to buy me a slushy, don't bother. I stopped liking those about twenty years ago."

He cast a scolding look at her. "Give me a little credit here."

"Sorry, I just can't think what else is down this road." In fact, they never drove this way—hadn't since their college days when they used to take this road out of town to their favorite make-out spot....

Could it be that Max was taking her there?

No way. She put the thought out of her head to keep from being disappointed when he pulled up in front of a tackle shop and announced they were going night-fishing or some other equally dense male idea of a surprise.

She settled into her seat and closed her eyes, still reeling from the evening at Juliet's house. Seeing all the effort that had been put into getting her and Max back together had touched her deeply, and no matter what happened between Juliet and Cole, Delia would always count Juliet as a good friend.

The images of the old video footage and the photos she hadn't had time to look at in years lingered in her mind, reminding her of the crazy, giddy feeling she used to get whenever Max entered the room. He'd always been outrageously handsome, the kind of guy women stopped to take a good, long look at, and Delia had found no small amount of pleasure in knowing he'd only had eyes for her.

Somehow, in all the craziness of raising their kids, she'd managed to forget how lucky she used to feel to be the woman Max loved—how lucky she used to feel that in all the world, she'd found her soul mate.

Gravel crunched under the car's tires, and it felt as if they'd gone off-road. Delia opened her eyes to see that they were on a gravel road, driving through the woods. It only took her a second to recognize the route to their old make-out spot. Her eyes welled up with tears, and she blinked them away.

"Are we going where I think we're going?"

"I've always thought we were using all this space in the Suburban for the wrong purpose. Instead of hauling around kids, we should be—"

"Max Matheson!" Delia stared at him, a burst of laughter threatening to escape her throat. "You're not suggesting we use the family SUV to make out, are you?"

"Babe, I'm planning to do a hell of a lot more than make out with you."

He pulled into a clearing—the same one they used to sit in years ago—and killed the engine. Delia felt warm and fuzzy from her eyebrows all the way down to where it counted most. She shifted in her seat and uncrossed her legs, suddenly all too aware of the friction from her tight jeans.

"Delia, baby, I'm sorry for the way I've let things slide between us. You deserve a hell of a lot more appreciation than you've been getting from me."

"I think we both can claim responsibility. I've been focused on the kids, you've been focused on the restaurant—life's just too busy."

"We need to fix that. I don't want the kids to leave home in a few years and then we suddenly find that we don't have anything left in common."

Delia realized then how dangerously close they'd come to letting that happen. "You're right. We need to make more time for us."

"I owe you a date night, at least every Saturday."

"But that's your busiest night at the restaurant."

"The assistant manager can handle it."

Delia sat back in her seat, stunned that Max was willing to make such a big sacrifice. For years, he'd rarely missed a Saturday night at the restaurant.

"But—"

"One more thing," he said, reaching over and taking her hand in his. "I'm ashamed of how messy the house has gotten. I promise me and the kids are going to pick up after ourselves from now on, and we'll *have* to, so the cleaning service I've hired can come in and clean every week."

Delia was speechless. Part of her hadn't believed the marriage strike would really work. "Thank you," she finally said. "That will be a huge help."

"It should have happened a long time ago."

Now she owed him a sacrifice of her own.

"And I owe you time for just the two of us at night. I know I tend to let the kids dominate my time in the evening, but I should be putting you first."

He smiled. "I'd like that."

Then he leaned over and kissed her, a soft kiss that hinted of pleasures to come.

"I have to admit, I've missed coming out here," she whispered. And she had, even though she hadn't realized it until tonight. She'd missed the sense of adventure, the romance of having a place where only the two of them went together.

"I've missed it, too. Now let's go try out that back seat."

A few minutes later, they'd managed to move the kids' junk and sports equipment out of the way enough to make good use of the second-row seats, and Delia couldn't remember the last time she'd felt so scandalous. For a girl who sported a rose tattoo on her inner thigh and who'd collected more than her share of Mardi Gras beads in her younger days, the realization of how safe and normal her life had become was a shock.

But she wouldn't trade her life now for her crazy younger days. She just wanted an occasional taste of adventure, and this was it. A little fun with her husband was what she'd been longing for without even realizing it.

She was about to climb into the back seat when Max stopped her. "Wait a minute, you're forgetting something."

Delia turned to him and wrapped her arms around him. "Yes?"

"I know it's cloudy out tonight, but aren't we supposed to wish on a star anyway?"

The tears came back to sting her eyes again. She'd completely forgotten about their silly little tradition—one they hadn't observed since before they'd had kids. Before making love under the stars, they'd always made a wish—world peace, multiple orgasms, a new car, anything was game. The goal wasn't so much to make the wish as it was to get the other person to laugh.

She smiled. "I wish for no state troopers to interrupt us tonight."

Max laughed at the memory of their long-ago brush with the law while making out here. "I wish for a lifetime of nights like this with you."

He slid his hands under her shirt then, and helped her out of it. A few minutes later, they were both unhindered by clothing, and Delia felt a whole new sense of appreciation for Max's devotion to keeping himself fit over the years. She'd always loved his body.

He lifted her up into the back seat, then bent to kiss her bare breast. She arched herself toward him and closed her eyes to savor the sweet sensations.

"You are more beautiful now than ever," he whispered. "I forget to tell you that."

Delia smiled, burying her fingers in his hair as he took one of her breasts into his mouth again. "Anything else you forget to tell me?"

He stopped and pulled her close. "I forget to tell you how much I appreciate that you're such a great mother, that you've made such a nice home for us, that you're more than I could've dared to hope for in a wife.''

In twenty years of marriage, she'd never heard him say those things before. She'd never been sure he noticed her hard work. She tried to swallow the lump that had formed in her throat.

When she could speak again, she said, ''Ditto.''

Max climbed into the back seat with her and closed the door, then reached up to the front seat to hit the auto-lock button for the doors.

Then he was on top of her, the hard familiar mass of his body covering her and thrilling her. He eased inside her and their bodies began to move like a perfectly choreographed dance. Even in the unfamiliar back seat, they knew each other's moves too well to make a misstep.

Max moved them toward their climax as only he could, and when they finally came, their bodies releasing at the same moment, Delia thanked her lucky stars that her little marriage strike had worked. She'd missed this, she'd missed her husband, and most of all, she'd missed the powerful force that had always pulled them together, that grew stronger the closer they came to each other, and that she vowed to herself she'd never question again.

HAVING TO SHOW UP at Max and Delia's anniversary party wasn't high on Cole's list of fun things to do, not after last night.

Cole had miscalculated Juliet's reaction in a big way. He'd known she cared about integrity, but he'd failed to anticipate just how violated she would feel by his lie. He'd never seen her so angry and hurt, and he had a feeling he'd created a wound in their relationship that wouldn't heal.

She'd been looking for a reason to run away, and he'd just handed her not one, but two, on a silver platter.

He was pretty sure his telling her he loved her had bothered her even more than the lie. And that, he should have been able to foresee. All his psychology training hadn't prepared him for Juliet, with her carefree attitude and her many hang-ups created by her aunt's eccentric philosophy.

He needed to come to terms with the fact that whatever he'd thought they had together was one-sided, and it was over.

Intellectually, he understood, but his heart hadn't quite accepted it. There was a raw place in his chest, and he'd spent last night and all day today trying to ignore it.

So walking into Juliet's house for the anniversary party would be a sheer act of will. He didn't want to be there, and he didn't want to see Juliet, but he also desperately wanted to see her. The house looked glorious in the evening light, its windows aglow with lamplight from within, its facade freshly painted and looking better than it had looked in years.

Cole went up the front steps and through the door without hesitating, willing himself to focus on Max and Delia's happiness and not Juliet.

Inside, a sizeable crowd had already gathered, and the room had the sort of warm festiveness Cole would always associate with Juliet. She knew how to throw a party, that was for sure.

"Cole, darling!"

He turned around to find his long-ago ex, Jeannie Monroe. Her presence baffled him momentarily, until he remembered that she and Delia were distant cousins, which would have warranted her getting an invitation to the party.

"Hi, Jeannie," he said, resisting his initial urge to flee the scene.

She was, after all, an attractive woman, and she could be a distraction from Juliet, maybe even a reminder to Juliet of what she'd missed out on.

No, he was above petty jealousy games. Sort of. Under normal circumstances. But nothing involving Juliet could be called normal circumstances. So yeah, maybe he did want to remind her of what she was missing. Even if he'd been in the wrong—and he certainly had—she could have given him a second chance.

"Where on earth have you been lately? I've tried to get in touch with you."

"Around. Didn't you get my voice mailbox?"

"I hate leaving messages—so impersonal. I've been wanting to invite you out on Daddy's new boat. It's a beauty."

Cole forced a smile, and when he spotted Juliet across the room, he felt like a scumbag for placing his hand on Jeannie's elbow, urging her a little closer so he could lean in and pretend that he needed to listen carefully over the din of the party.

"I'd love to go out on the boat sometime," he heard himself saying. It was a flat-out lie, and he began to wonder if Juliet's reaction hadn't been so out of line.

Maybe he didn't deserve a second chance after all.

The house quickly filled up with Max and Delia's family and friends, and Cole forced himself to endure Jeannie's company for most of the night, trying his best to be open to the idea of enjoying her.

Which was stupid, considering his chest was still suffering a gaping wound from Juliet.

Max caught him at the bar getting a drink. "Hey, what's with you and Jeannie? I thought you were dating Juliet."

Cole shrugged, not ready to reveal the sordid details of his love life. "Juliet and I aren't seeing each other."

"But last night—"

"Was purely an effort to get you and Delia back together."

Max smiled a mysterious smile. "It sure as hell worked, let me tell you. I owe you both a big thanks."

"It was all Juliet's idea."

"She seems like a great girl. I can't believe you let her get away, little brother." Max clapped Cole's shoulder and wandered off.

He couldn't believe he'd let her get away, either, but he had. And he understood now that they'd never been meant to be in the first place. If they had been, then Juliet would have returned his feelings, plain and simple.

Plain, simple, and incredibly painful.

THIS WAS THE MOST miserable Juliet had ever been at a party. Not that things weren't going smoothly. The house was aglow and more beautiful than she could ever remember it looking, Finn's catering was a hit and the guests were mingling and having what looked to be a fabulous time. One guest in particular was having a much better time than she would have liked.

She forced herself not to glance in Cole's direction again. He'd spent the entire evening flirting with the woman Juliet remembered from his birthday party that he'd tried so hard to avoid—the woman with a look of unabashed lust in her eyes—and Juliet wanted to kick herself for feeling so jealous.

Wasn't this what she wanted? Hadn't she resisted Cole's advances toward a serious relationship every step of the way? And hadn't she kicked him out of her house last night with the conviction that they were over for good?

Deep down, she understood the real problem. She'd allowed herself to get too close to him, and emotions had gotten involved. Messy, unreliable emotions. She'd succumbed to the dangers of romance, and now she was suffering the consequences. All her rules for a carefree love life were in place for a reason, and when she violated them, she suffered.

She and Cole were over for good. It would just take a while to clean up the mess and get back to the uncomplicated existence she craved.

"Jule, we need to talk."

She looked up from the platter of miniquiches she'd been staring a bit too intently at and found herself face to face with Delia. Delia, who'd so quickly become her dear friend and who had an uncanny knack for knowing what was really going on. She was the last person Juliet wanted to talk to right now.

"I'm, uh, just trying to decide if we need more quiches on the table."

"The finger foods can wait. No one's going to starve with all this food you have out." Delia slipped her hand around Juliet's wrist and tugged her toward the kitchen.

"But—"

"No buts. You're coming with me."

Juliet hated discussing emotional issues, especially when *her* emotions were the ones under scrutiny. "So do you like the party?"

"It's lovely, thank you. Now tell me what's going on between you and Cole."

That was an easy answer. "Absolutely nothing."

Delia pinned her with a glare. "A week ago you two were an item, and now you're working so hard to avoid each other it's making me tired just watching you."

Juliet fiddled with a dish towel until Delia snatched it out of her hand.

"I'm waiting for an answer," she said.

"I know you had high hopes, but the truth is—and Cole knew it all along—I'm not interested in a serious relationship. I just wanted to have a little fun, and I'm sorry if anyone got hurt. That wasn't my intention."

Delia frowned, then reached for Juliet's hand and held it between hers. "It looks like you're the one who got hurt, Jule."

"Yeah, Cole seems to be enjoying himself just fine," Juliet said, surprised at the spiteful tone her voice had taken.

"It's an act, I can tell. He hasn't been interested in my cousin, Jeannie, in years, and he isn't now, either."

"How can you be so sure?" she asked and immediately regretted it. Wasn't she supposed to be cool, aloof, and unconcerned about his love life?

"I see him looking everywhere in the room but at you, until he's sure you're not looking, and then he casts furtive little glances your way."

"Regardless, it's over between us. He lied to me, and I don't tolerate liars."

"Lied about what?"

"You'll have to ask him that. Let's just say our whole relationship was based on a false pretense."

Delia cocked one eyebrow. "That doesn't sound like Cole."

"He's a better actor than you think, then." .

Delia still looked doubtful, but she didn't argue any further. "Thank you for this party," she said. "I can't tell you how much it means to me—"

"Don't say another word. It's my pleasure, especially seeing how happy you two look tonight."

Delia sighed. "Yeah, well, you should have seen us last night, after we left your house."

Juliet smiled. She might have been absolutely miserable, but at least the people who mattered most were having a good time. "I wish you both another twenty years—and another twenty after that—of wedded bliss."

The kitchen door swung open, and she caught sight of Cole and Jeannie, smiling and laughing together. Her stomach clenched, and she wanted to run away and cry.

Delia and Max could keep their wedded bliss. Juliet would take alone, carefree, and uncomplicated any day.

15

---

*The League of Scandalous Women's Guiding Principle 15:
A scandalous woman never forgets that she is a
woman, with a woman's needs and desires. She
honors her own heart's desires above all else.*

IF THE GROUP OF WOMEN laughing and talking in the formal
parlor was any indication, the first meeting of the League
of Scandalous Women was a big success. Juliet came back
from the kitchen and placed a refill tray of finger foods on
the cocktail table, then sat down next to Audrey and Rebecca, who were chatting about Rebecca's upcoming wedding.

Audrey was looking more pregnant by the day, and Juliet
was surprised she'd even made the meeting, considering
her due date was two days ago.

When there was a lull in the conversation, Juliet asked,
"How are you feeling?"

Audrey rolled her eyes and flashed a tired smile. "Like
I've been invaded by a watermelon."

"Well, you look great, especially for someone who's two
days past due," Juliet said, and she was surprised to realize
she meant it.

Just yesterday, she'd passed a pregnant woman on the
sidewalk and had found herself admiring some unnamable

quality about the woman. She'd finally understood why people reached out and fondled pregnant women's bellies. And while she didn't actually want to *be* pregnant, she could appreciate the condition for the amazing thing that it was.

"You're a terrible liar," Audrey said, then laughed.

"I'm not lying!"

"She's right," Rebecca chimed in. "Seeing you like this makes me wonder how I'll look when I'm knocked up."

"I'm sure you'll be the sexiest pregnant babe around," Audrey said.

Juliet marveled at the fact that she wasn't even getting weirded out by the conversation. Rebecca, pregnant, would have been unimaginable to her two months ago, but now it seemed almost inevitable.

Juliet had planned for there to be a formal discussion segment of their meeting, but so far, everyone had been so busy chatting, it had seemed a shame to interrupt. She looked around the room, listening for a lull in the conversation. What she saw was a diverse group of women exchanging ideas and having fun.

The dull ache she'd been feeling since the anniversary party over the weekend had magically disappeared in the past hour, and she actually felt happy. Though if she allowed her thoughts to touch on Cole, even for a moment, the happiness vanished. She shoved aside the negative thoughts and focused on her friends.

Delia was sitting across the room talking to a member of Juliet's former party crowd. It amazed her how much getting to know Delia had changed her perspective on so many things. In Delia, she finally had an example of cool motherhood, of a woman who'd managed to settle down without giving up an important part of herself in the process.

And as she looked around the room, she realized she could probably say the same thing about all of her friends who'd gotten married and had kids. They were all still cool, interesting women—and maybe she'd allowed a barrier to form between them because she'd felt left behind.

"You're looking wistful," Rebecca said.

Juliet smiled. "Want to help me refill the coffee?"

"Sure." Rebecca helped her gather the coffeepots and carry them back to the kitchen. When they were alone, she said, "So what's with your quiet mood today?"

Juliet almost denied it, but she was dying to talk to someone who cared. "I guess I've been a bit of a wreck ever since Delia and Max's anniversary party."

"You saw Cole there?"

"And it was awful. I didn't expect to feel like this," Juliet said as she made more coffee.

Rebecca frowned. "I'm still shocked you broke up with him."

"I told you I wasn't interested in a relationship."

"I thought you were just in denial, that you'd figure out you were happier with Cole than without him."

Was that true? *Was* she happier with Cole? It seemed impossible that she could be happier tied down than free to do as she pleased, and yet…

Maybe this was just the consequence of getting involved when she knew she shouldn't have. She'd broken the rules of a carefree fling, and now she was paying for it. She'd been a fool to think she could have a fling with a guy like Cole without more than her body getting involved.

Juliet scrambled to think of an intelligent way to explain

why she hadn't wanted more from Cole. "You know how I feel about long-term relationships. They're messy, emotional—someone always gets hurt."

"For someone as fun-loving as you, I find it hard to believe that you consider avoiding emotional entanglements your number one priority in life. Look at all you'll miss out on."

"If I want to get involved, I'll pick someone easier to deal with than Cole. He's a psychologist, for heaven's sake!"

"So?"

"So he was constantly analyzing my every dysfunctional action, constantly using psychobabble as a barrier between us."

Rebecca looked unconvinced. "Why would he do that? He was clearly crazy about you."

"Because he's as screwed up as anyone else. He just hides it behind lots of big words."

"Then you can be screwed up together. Just like everyone else."

Juliet watched coffee drip down into the pot, trying to imagine herself happy with Cole. She'd avoided trying to picture it before. It seemed like the kind of fairy-tale silliness her aunt would have declared unworthy of a modern girl like Juliet.

And especially at the first meeting of the new League of Scandalous Women, it was entirely inappropriate.

"If I want a boyfriend, I'll choose someone who acts like a guy, not like a psychologist."

Rebecca was still frowning, looking at her as if she was throwing away the opportunity of a lifetime.

She was wrong. Juliet only had to think of how miserable she'd felt in the past week to know that.

"If that's how you feel, okay. I didn't realize he was such an obnoxious guy."

Juliet should have protested. Obnoxious was too strong a word. Cole wasn't even remotely obnoxious. But she couldn't bring herself to defend him, not when it would make her sound crazier than she already feared she was sounding. What she'd said about Cole was true. He really had erected a barrier of psychobabble between them, for whatever reason, she wasn't sure.

Maybe she'd been to blame.

Maybe he understood even better than she did that she'd hurt him in the end, and psychology was his only defense.

The sick feeling returned to her belly, and she had the sudden urge to go hide in her bedroom.

"I'm sorry," Rebecca said. "I shouldn't have brought this up right now. We're supposed to be having girl time. Let's get this coffee back out there before someone starts dancing on your antiques."

Juliet forced herself to smile. Rebecca was right—this was their day to enjoy their friends, not wallow in angst over guy troubles.

They refilled the coffeepots with fresh coffee and brought them back to the parlor. Juliet cleared her throat to get everyone's attention, then waited for her friends to quiet down.

"Thank you for being a part of our meeting tonight," she said. "The League of Scandalous Women stands for sisterhood, for self-expression and individuality, for the celebration of women breaking down barriers."

"The only barrier I've been breaking down lately is the

plastic one between me and my miniature candy bars," Audrey said, and everyone laughed.

"Over the next few months, I'd like us to center the formal part of our meetings around discussing the guiding principles of our newly formed group. They were established about forty years ago when the original League was formed, and I think they're just as appropriate today as they were back then."

She retrieved a stack of papers from a nearby table and passed them around.

"Let's discuss the first guiding principle, which has nothing to do with chocolate, unfortunately," she said, casting a teasing glance at Audrey.

Rebecca read it aloud. "A scandalous woman knows that brazenness is a virtue."

Juliet had spent most of her life living with that principle in mind. It hadn't helped her with Cole—and it had in fact gotten her in the predicament she'd so badly wanted to avoid. She'd been as brazen as she pleased, stripping for him in front of an audience, taking him to bed and making love to him all night long....

Delia spoke up, saving Juliet from her own thoughts. "So what examples can we come up with to illustrate how it pays to be a brazen hussy in our everyday lives?"

Laughter at Delia's comment instantly loosened everyone up. "Considering my current boatlike condition," Audrey said, "I might never get laid if I didn't just tell my husband what I want."

When the laughter died down again, Rebecca said, "How about in less obvious situations? For instance, I had this situation at work..."

Juliet listened, feeling more wistful than she would have

liked. Why had brazenness failed her? She felt like a failure as a scandalous woman, but as she looked around the room, she realized that if she'd failed, she was happy at least to be surrounded by women who'd love her regardless.

That was a lot to be thankful for.

JULIET HADN'T FELT LIKE eating in days. An entire week had passed since the anniversary party, and she couldn't remember the last time she'd had a full meal. Even at the League of Scandalous Women's first meeting yesterday, she'd been uninterested in the finger foods—normally her favorite things to eat.

She stared into her nearly empty pantry at the few forlorn cans of fruit and the old container of oatmeal and realized she still wasn't that hungry. Instead of eating breakfast, she opted for a cup of coffee.

The kitchen was cluttered with coffee cups and plates from last night's meeting. The evening had been a success from start to finish. They'd had a lively discussion on the first few guiding principles, and everyone had seemed eager to meet up again next month.

All in all, Juliet should have been thrilled. She now had many of her old friends committed to getting together once a month, and she'd revived one of her favorite pieces of Ophelia's colorful history.

But she didn't feel thrilled. She felt like nothing was right, like her life had made a serious wrong turn, and she couldn't find her way back to a familiar neighborhood.

Juliet carried her cup of coffee to the attic, where she planned to spend the day cleaning, sorting through old junk, clearing out the only place left in the house that needed attention.

She couldn't remember ever having felt so pitiful in her life. It wasn't her nature to mope and feel sorry for herself. Yet here she was, in an absolutely miserable state.

She should have been happy not just about the League of Scandalous Women, but about everything. Renovations on the house were nearly finished, she'd all but closed her aunt's estate, her business was thriving now that she'd set it up in the new location.

Her life was about as good as it could get, wasn't it?

Wasn't it?

Damn Cole and his theory of sexual relativity. Not only had he ruined her plan to have a little carefree fun, but he'd ruined her chances of ever having another carefree fling again. Now that she'd seen the painful side effects, how could she ever fall into bed with another man?

And would she ever want to? She supposed it was a good thing to lose her addiction to men now, as it would serve her well in her spinsterhood. Ophelia never had approved of the way she loved dating, so her aunt was probably pleased to be looking down on her now to see that she'd finally learned the peril of reckless romance.

She set her cup of coffee down on an old chest and looked around, wondering where to start. Discarded lamps, old toys, boxes of linens, antiquated radios and other pieces of junk... She decided to start sorting things by categories—to be thrown away, given away and taken to an antique dealer—and opened up a nearby trunk, curious to see what was inside.

It was filled with white satin fabric, and when Juliet carefully took it out, she discovered that the fabric was actually a wedding dress. A delicate, beautiful old dress in a tiny size that could only have been made for her aunt.

For Ophelia?

She frowned and stared at it. Ophelia had always told her she'd never been married, and Juliet had certainly never found any marriage documents in the estate.

Ophelia hadn't worn this dress, had she? But if not, then whose was it?

She carefully set aside the dress on the cleanest surface she could find, then looked in the trunk again. Inside was an antique pair of white satin shoes, matching gloves, and a veil. And in one corner of the trunk was a journal. She picked it up and opened it, and immediately recognized Ophelia's flamboyant penmanship.

The date on the first page of the journal would have made her aunt eighteen years old, and it began with the sentence, "I met him at the spring dance."

Juliet read the description of Ophelia's meeting a man named Charlie, who was ten years older than herself, of the way he'd charmed her and danced the night away with her, and how he'd asked to see her again. The tone of the first entry was different than in her aunt's later journals. The girl who'd written this had perhaps been less sure of herself, more idealistic, more excited about the possibilities that lay ahead of her.

She closed the journal and stared at the tapestry cover, not sure if she wanted to read on. Reading Ophelia's other journals had always felt like reading published memoirs—she'd written them for an audience, for whoever cared to read her thoughts on life.

But this…this had been written for a different purpose.

Inside this journal were the dreams of the girl her aunt had been, and Juliet felt like a voyeur peeking in at them. She blinked away an unwelcome dampness in her eyes and took a deep breath of the musty attic air, trying to ignore the smell of mothballs and old junk. Voyeur or not, part of her desperately wanted to know this other side of her aunt, wanted a glimpse of her before she'd become the formidable woman Juliet had known.

Carefully, and with butterflies flitting around in her belly, she opened the journal again and began to read. An hour later, she hadn't moved from her spot on the attic floor. Her back ached, her legs were stiff, and when she stopped reading, she realized she had tears leaking from the corners of her eyes.

She'd read of her aunt's courtship with the man she'd met at the dance, Charles Cantrell. He'd swept her off her feet and courted her like a devoted puppy, and she'd adored him in a way Juliet would never have guessed Ophelia capable of. They'd courted for a year before becoming engaged, but they'd agreed to put off their wedding until Ophelia could finish college.

Charlie had been in the army reserves, and while Ophelia was in her junior year of college, his unit had been activated, notified that they would deploy to the war in Korea.

The two had planned a hasty wedding, but Charlie was called away even earlier than expected, and their wedding never happened.

Ophelia had been furious at first but had finally accepted the situation. She wrote of how she admired his bravery and of her fear for his safety. Later, she wrote of having received a letter from him after he'd survived the battle to recapture Seoul, and Juliet had turned the page to see that there was only one entry after that.

She'd closed the book, afraid to read what came next. She could guess. But after sitting for a few minutes unable to keep reading, curiosity finally got the best of her. She had to find out what had helped shape her aunt into the woman she'd known.

Juliet opened the book to the last page that had an entry, and began to read.

A letter came last week from Charlie's parents, a letter I've both dreaded and expected since the day he left for the war.

He died during an ambush on his convoy, and they say he fought bravely to the end, though that hardly matters to me. If it meant I could have him back, I would have preferred he flee like a coward, but imagining what might have been is senseless.

The dreams I held dear of our future together seem foolish now, and I know that this world is no place for the soft-hearted girl I once was.

Juliet flipped through the empty pages that followed, blinking away tears. She'd never known about her aunt's first love. Ophelia had never even hinted that she'd loved a man so dearly and lost him in the war.

Now there was this new piece of the puzzle of Ophelia's life, one that answered questions Juliet had never even thought to ask.

She stood up from the attic floor and stretched her aching limbs, then picked up her forgotten cup of coffee and headed downstairs for a refill. The questions nagged at her—why had Ophelia never mentioned this first love? Had Charlie's death turned her bitter for the rest of her life? Were those the experiences that had shaped her entire outlook?

All the advice Ophelia had given her over the years looked different when considered in the light of her tragic first love. Not always so much avant-garde as it was jaded. She was not the woman Juliet had thought she'd known, and she'd never cared enough to show her who she really was.

Juliet thought of what Rebecca had told her about how Ophelia had showed her a melancholy side Juliet had never seen. Why couldn't she show that side of herself to her own niece—to the child she might as well have called her daughter?

Loneliness stabbed her in the gut. She ached for someone to hold her close and comfort her, treat her like a little girl for just a few brief moments, let her cry and then wipe away her tears.

Juliet couldn't remember the last time she'd cried for her mother or father, but now she thought of them and the dam broke. She collapsed on the stairs and pressed her face against the railing, let her tears dampen the wood. Why hadn't Ophelia ever encouraged her to do this? To let it all out?

It was too late to ask now. But it wasn't too late to reconsider how much she should let her aunt's philosophy shape her decisions. Ophelia had been a smart woman, and she'd had some good ideas, but that didn't mean that she was always right.

She thought of Cole, of the way he made her feel, of the choices she'd made in their relationship. And she realized she'd been letting Ophelia do the decision-making.

Ophelia, who'd had her tender young heart broken and never repaired. Ophelia, who'd held everyone at arm's length for the rest of her life, afraid of being hurt again.

Ophelia, who'd raised her to believe romantic love was a fairy-tale notion unbefitting a modern woman.

Juliet stood up and went to the kitchen. She dumped the cold coffee into the sink and poured herself a new cup, topped it off with milk, then drank the entire cup. She needed the caffeine to help her think more clearly, now that she knew she needed to figure out what *she* believed, not what her aunt had raised her to believe.

And what *did* she believe?

Juliet thought of Cole again. The way he made her feel—thrilled, content, loved, safe, desired.

Happy.

Even with his endless psychobabble, he made her happy.

She thought of all her previous relationships, of her fruitless pursuit of the perfect carefree fling. She'd never managed to feel before the way she felt with Cole.

Because she was in love with Cole.

The idea struck her like a bolt of lightning, and she had no idea what to do with it. She had no idea if she wanted all that came along with being in love—the commitment, the vulnerability, the possibility of being broken the way Ophelia had been.

She stared out the kitchen window at the freshly tamed and cultivated garden. The top of the gazebo where she'd made love to Cole peeked out above the greenery, and she thought of their night together there and all their days and nights together. She'd felt more alive with Cole than she'd ever felt before.

She might not have been carefree, but she'd been happy on a whole new level.

And she was ready to give up carefree for happy.

When she thought of the love her aunt had lost, she knew

she wanted Cole and all the risks and rewards that came with him. She wanted him in her life, if he would still give her a chance.

Now she needed to ask him for forgiveness.

COLE HAD POSSIBLY just completed one of the most uninspired teaching sessions of his career. The truth was, he'd been doing everything halfheartedly, living his life with the enthusiasm of a slug.

It had to stop.

"And don't forget, read chapters ten through twenty of the text by Thursday," Cole said to the class as students began stuffing notebooks into backpacks and shuffling down the center aisle toward the door. He watched the classroom empty and found himself wondering if he'd ever really enjoy his life again.

He sighed at his own doomsday thoughts, the sort of which he'd been having far too often.

"Dr. Matheson?"

Cole turned his attention to the male student hovering next to his lectern. "Yes?"

"Could you, um, take a glance at my paper and give me a little feedback on it?"

Cole nodded and took the paper, then scanned it for a minute before the sight of someone entering the classroom caught his eye. He glanced up at the lone figure, and his stomach clenched when he realized it was Juliet.

She flashed a tentative smile and waved, then sat down at one of the desks in the back of the room. Cole took that as a sign that she wasn't there to ask him for help on her homework. But he wasn't sure he was ready to face her again and deal with the ensuing emotions that would be stirred up.

"If you can stop by my office tomorrow evening, I can have this read and marked with revision comments by then," Cole said to the student at his side.

When he was alone with Juliet, she cleared her throat and stood up. "Dr. Matheson?"

"Juliet." He wanted to run up the aisle and take her in his arms, hold her tight and never let her go, but what would be the point now? The very impulse was enough to bring back the raw, empty feeling that kept him wide awake at night, aching for sleep, aching to forget.

"I have a little presentation, if you're willing to listen."

He was intrigued, but he knew better than to get his hopes up now, after Juliet had proved herself incapable of having a serious relationship.

He shrugged. "Sure, I can listen."

"If you'll have a seat," she said, motioning to the front row of desks.

Cole sat down in one of the chairs and folded down the desktop to rest his arm on, while Juliet approached the lectern and took her place there.

"I'll be presenting an oral report of my findings in our research of the Theory of Sexual Relativity." She flipped through a few index cards before beginning, while Cole tried to figure out exactly where she was going with this.

And then she continued. "Test Subject Number One, Juliet, while initially resistant to the idea of emotional intimacy connected to a sexual relationship, was slowly won over to the concept.

"In fact, over time she began to see the error of her ways

with regard to casual sex, and she developed significant feelings for Test Subject Number Two, Cole Matheson.''

Cole shifted in his seat, more intrigued now but still wary. ''Significant feelings'' was a far cry from a profession of love.

''What sort of significant feelings did Test Subject Number One develop?''

''She first experienced feelings of denial and confusion, but once allowed time for reflection, she began to see clearly that she'd fallen in love with Test Subject Number Two.''

''In love? Is she sure of it?'' Cole asked, his entire body tensed. He'd given up hoping Juliet would come around, and he couldn't settle for anything less than all of her. He didn't want her as just a lover or a friend.

He wanted all of her—lover, friend, companion—and if she was here to ask for anything less, he'd tell her to leave and not come back.

''She's sure of it, and she's very sorry for not coming to her senses sooner.''

''Test Subject Number Two is extremely happy with this new development.''

Juliet smiled and swiped at the corner of her eye. Was she actually crying? No way, not Juliet. ''Test Subject Number One is ready to give up her misguided notions about love and sex. She admits that the Theory of Sexual Relativity does indeed have merit. I believe her exact thoughts on the subject are, 'My emotional health has suffered a serious negative impact thanks to my previous unwillingness to have anything more than sex with Test Subject Number Two.'''

Previous? A tightness in his throat kept Cole from speaking for a few moments.

What he wanted to say was that he loved Juliet and didn't plan on letting her go again.

"I'm sorry, Cole," she said, her student presentation voice gone now. "I know it took me a little too long to figure it out, but I love you."

Cole knew for sure then—Juliet was The One, and he didn't mean as in test subject. He watched her come out from behind the lectern and approach him, her steps tentative, her gaze full of uncertainty.

He stood up and went to her, meeting her halfway down the aisle, and he took her in his arms. This time, he wouldn't let her get away.

"If I could relive every moment since we first met and make different choices along the way, I would."

"Are you sure you want this?" he asked, unwilling to accept anything less than all of her.

"Absolutely," she said, and the uncertainty disappeared from her eyes.

"Sure enough to marry me?"

She started laughing, and tears spilled over the rims of her eyes. Cole kissed away the dampness.

"Are you proposing?" she said when she recovered.

He dipped his head down and kissed her, soft and slow. He intended to make her forget everything except the two of them, then and there. "I am," he finally whispered when he broke the kiss.

No matter what else happened in his life from that point on, Cole knew he'd never be happy unless he knew he'd given his all for Juliet. Maybe she didn't want marriage, but he had to ask.

She stared at him, her eyes wide and searching. "Yes," she said. "I'm sure."

Cole smiled and kissed her again, then lifted her up and carried her down the aisle, out of the classroom, out of the building and into the common area, where students turned to gawk as he headed for his car. They had lots of making up to do, and life with Juliet was a party Cole wouldn't have missed for anything.

Epilogue

One Month Later

"I'VE ALWAYS WANTED to do it with a sexy bridesmaid," Cole said as he cornered Juliet in the hotel elevator.

He pinned her against the wall and kissed her until she'd completely forgotten where she'd been going.

She was pretty sure she could disappear from Rebecca's wedding reception for a short while without anyone missing her—and if they did miss her, too bad. No way was she missing out on this.

The wedding had been perfect, and the reception was rolling along beautifully. One less flapper girl bridesmaid for twenty minutes or so wasn't going to spoil the fun.

"Do you have any idea how to stop one of these things?" she asked, nodding to the elevator's control panel.

Cole smiled, pushed a button, and the elevator stopped. Then he produced a handkerchief, reached up and covered the lens of the security camera with it.

"Isn't an alarm or something going to go off?"

"I guess we'd better be quick then," he said, getting right to the business of lifting up her skirt and pulling down her panties. "Mmm, thigh-high stockings. Very sexy."

"I thought you'd like them."

He lifted her onto the handrail and rested her there as he

opened his fly. A moment later, he was inside her, and Juliet sighed at the sweet, familiar feel of him.

"Great job on the reception, by the way," he said.

"Could we talk later? We're on the clock here."

"Problem is, all this wedding festivity has me thinking about our wedding, and when it's going to happen."

Juliet squirmed, aching for him to get down to business. "January twentieth, remember? That's the date we agreed on."

"Not good enough. I'm thinking Rebecca and Alec had the right idea when they moved their wedding date up."

"Our wedding date's less than three months from now. How much sooner do you want?" She tightened her legs around his hips, hoping he'd get the message, though she did feel flattered that he was in such a hurry to marry her.

"I'm thinking a Christmas Eve wedding. I want us to spend the holidays married, not engaged."

A Christmas Eve wedding?

It was a little last-minute, but it sounded very romantic, and she had perfected her efficient-wedding-planning techniques with Rebecca's wedding.

Juliet had other more urgent things on her mind though, like the ache for Cole that was growing with each second that passed.

He made no move to respond to all her urging, and she began to understand his tactic. "This is cruel, you know—trying to coerce me by withholding sex."

He glanced down at their bodies joined together. "You can hardly call this withholding."

"You know what I mean," she said, breathless now.

"Just think, we could ring in the New Year on our honeymoon."

She took a deep breath. A few months ago, diving into marriage headfirst would have scared the hell out of her. Now she was amazed not to feel even the slightest trepidation at the thought of moving up their wedding date.

She smiled. "Someplace sunny and tropical, with our own private bungalow?"

"Of course."

"Then I think I can handle a Christmas Eve wedding."

He kissed her, a deep, lingering kiss that thrilled her down to her toes, and then he got on with what he'd started.

Juliet clung to him, thankful that she'd found her heart's greatest desire—the one she was willing to risk it all for. It was like Guiding Principle 15 said: A scandalous woman never forgets that she's a woman, with a woman's needs and desires…. And Cole Matheson fulfilled them all.

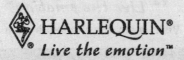

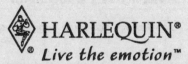

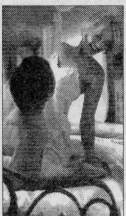

Single in South Beach

Nightlife on the Strip just got a little hotter!

Join author Joanne Rock as she takes you back to Miami Beach and its hottest singles' playground. Club Paradise has staked its claim in the decadent South Beach nightlife and the women in charge are determined to keep the sexy resort on top. So what will they do with the hot men who show up at the club?

GIRL GONE WILD
Harlequin Blaze #135
May 2004

DATE WITH A DIVA
Harlequin Blaze #139
June 2004

HER FINAL FLING
Harlequin Temptation #983
July 2004

Don't miss the continuation of this red-hot series from Joanne Rock!
Look for these books at your favorite retail outlet.

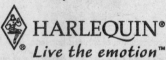